"How about making a little noise?" Boone whispered to the woman on the bed. "You know, so the real *bad guys will think you're enjoying yourself?"*

"I will *not!*" she said indignantly.

He grabbed her wrist, and she squealed. Then he dragged her closer, and she squealed again. "That's good."

But it *wasn't* good. She was breathing hard, as if they were really making love. Her green eyes were fiery and latched to his. And he couldn't stop wishing for what he was only pretending to do. "One more time, sugar."

"Don't call me—"

He hauled her off the bed so that she came to her feet and ran smack-dab into his bare chest. This time she screamed, and Boone let go of her.

She glanced up at him suspiciously.

He couldn't resist. "Was it good for you, too?" he whispered.

Dear Reader,

The warm weather is upon us, and things are heating up to match here at Silhouette Intimate Moments. Candace Camp returns to A LITTLE TOWN IN TEXAS with *Smooth-Talking Texan*, featuring another of her fabulous Western heroes. Town sheriff Quinn Sutton is one irresistible guy—as attorney Lisa Mendoza is about to learn.

We're now halfway through ROMANCING THE CROWN, our suspenseful royal continuity. In Valerie Parv's *Royal Spy*, a courtship of convenience quickly becomes the real thing—but is either the commoner or the princess what they seem? Marie Ferrarella begins THE BACHELORS OF BLAIR MEMORIAL with *In Graywolf's Hands*, featuring a Native American doctor and the FBI agent who ends up falling for him. Linda Winstead Jones is back with *In Bed With Boone,* a thrillingly romantic kidnapping story—of course with a happy ending. Then go *Beneath the Silk* with author Wendy Rosnau, whose newest is sensuous and suspenseful, and completely enthralling. Finally, welcome brand-new author Catherine Mann. *Wedding at White Sands* is her first book, but we've already got more—including an exciting trilogy—lined up from this talented newcomer.

Enjoy all six of this month's offerings, then come back next month for even more excitement as Intimate Moments continues to present some of the best romance reading you'll find anywhere.

Leslie J. Wainger
Executive Senior Editor

Please address questions and book requests to:
Silhouette Reader Service
U.S.: 3010 Walden Ave., P.O. Box 1325, Buffalo, NY 14269
Canadian: P.O. Box 609, Fort Erie, Ont. L2A 5X3

In Bed with Boone

LINDA
WINSTEAD
JONES

Silhouette

INTIMATE MOMENTS™

Published by Silhouette Books

America's Publisher of Contemporary Romance

SILHOUETTE BOOKS

ISBN 0-373-27226-X

IN BED WITH BOONE

Copyright © 2002 by Linda Winstead Jones

All rights reserved. Except for use in any review, the reproduction or utilization of this work in whole or in part in any form by any electronic, mechanical or other means, now known or hereafter invented, including xerography, photocopying and recording, or in any information storage or retrieval system, is forbidden without the written permission of the editorial office, Silhouette Books, 300 East 42nd Street, New York, NY 10017 U.S.A.

All characters in this book have no existence outside the imagination of the author and have no relation whatsoever to anyone bearing the same name or names. They are not even distantly inspired by any individual known or unknown to the author, and all incidents are pure invention.

This edition published by arrangement with Harlequin Books S.A.

® and TM are trademarks of Harlequin Books S.A., used under license. Trademarks indicated with ® are registered in the United States Patent and Trademark Office, the Canadian Trade Marks Office and in other countries.

Visit Silhouette at www.eHarlequin.com

Printed in U.S.A.

Books by Linda Winstead Jones

Silhouette Intimate Moments

LINDA WINSTEAD JONES

would rather write than do anything else. Since she cannot cook, gave up ironing many years ago and finds cleaning the house a complete waste of time, she has plenty of time to devote to her obsession with writing. Occasionally she's tried to expand her horizons by taking classes. In the past she's taken instruction on yoga, French (a dismal failure), Chinese cooking, cake decorating (food-related classes are always a good choice, even for someone who can't cook), belly dancing (trust me, this was a long time ago) and, of course, creative writing.

She lives in Huntsville, Alabama, with her husband of more years than she's willing to admit and the youngest of their three sons.

She can be reached via www.eHarlequin.com or her own Web site www.lindawinsteadjones.com.

This book is dedicated, with much love,
to my New York friends. You've all been very much
on my mind as I finish this story, and I continue
to be amazed by your heart and courage.
For Matrice and Diane, Leslie and Lynda.
For Chris and Brooke and Tim.
For Joanna, Amy and Richard.

Chapter 1

A blind date was a sure sign of a life gone wrong. Jayne Barrington stared out the passenger-side window of the speeding Mercedes and wondered where *her* life had gone wrong. The Arizona landscape, so different from her Mississippi home, provided no answers. Giving in to the only sign of nervousness she ever allowed herself, Jayne fingered the pearls that hung at her throat.

She expected too much, she imagined. The kind of man she dreamed about was long gone. A gentleman. A gallant. A knight in shining armor. Those men didn't exist anymore.

"I must've taken a wrong turn," Jim said nervously. "Surely there's a road that cuts through to the south. We'll be at the party in no time at all." The false note of cheer he tried to put into his voice didn't quite work.

They hadn't passed a house or a streetlight for miles. Jim had driven by the last gas station twenty minutes ago. When Jayne had suggested that he stop and ask for directions, he'd uttered a valiant rejection of her sensible idea. *Men.*

The car jerked as the narrow asphalt road ended and without warning they found themselves on what was little more than a dirt trail.

"Turn the car around," Jayne insisted in her frostiest voice. "This road can't possibly go anywhere."

Jim leaned forward and craned his long scrawny neck to see over the steering wheel, peering at the small section of the road his headlights illuminated. "There's a ditch on this side. I'm afraid if I try to turn around here, we'll get stuck. Keep your eye out for a nice flat place to turn around."

For the past half hour, everything had been flat! Jayne took a deep breath in and exhaled slowly. Pamela would pay dearly for setting up this disastrous date. Jim might be relatively handsome—but for that long and skinny neck—and he definitely ran in the correct social circles; but the man was dumb. Beneath that pretty face and the expensive dental work, he had fewer working brain cells than the average twelve-year-old. Jayne could abide many faults in a man, but stupidity wasn't one of them.

They'd left Flagstaff two hours ago, eventually leaving behind the pine forests for stretches of flat land broken here and there by magnificent red rock formations and scruffy plants that fought to survive in the harsh dirt. They should have reached their destination more than half an hour ago, but she hadn't seen any of the landmarks she'd been told to look for.

For goodness' sake, they were completely lost!

"I think I see lights," Jim said, a twinge of hopeful optimism in his voice.

Jayne looked ahead, and sure enough a soft glow broke the complete darkness of the night in the distance. Not enough to be the headlights of an approaching car or a house situated here in the middle of nowhere, but more illumination than a flashlight would give off. A distinct uneasiness settled in her stomach. Who knew what might be ahead?

"Perhaps you should just put the car in reverse and back up until we hit the asphalt, and then you can turn around," Jayne said sensibly. "To be honest, I've developed a headache. Let's forget the party. I just want to go back to the hotel." Her father would be disappointed, but there was just so much a dutiful daughter could do to further a promising political career. Jim had been looking forward to the party at Hollywood producer Corbin Marsh's secluded Arizona home. He had a notion that if Marsh got a good look at his pretty face, he'd soon be a star.

"Drive backward all that way?" Jim shot her an astonished glance. "It'll be easier to just find a wide place to turn around. If we don't come across a good spot by the time we get to whatever that light ahead is, I'll try to back up." He tried for a reassuring smile. "I was really looking forward to meeting Marsh, but if you insist, we can forget the party and go back to your hotel. I'm sure he'll want to meet with you at another time, and I'll just tag along then."

No way was she inviting this moron into her hotel room, and this was definitely their last date. There was no way he would be "tagging along" with her anywhere! But now, while she was at his mercy practically in the middle of nowhere, was probably not the time to tell him so.

The glow ahead grew brighter, and soon Jayne was able to make out dimly lit forms moving about two cars that had been pulled off the road. Three or four powerful flashlights lit the night, illuminating the scene, a scene that struck her as not being quite right. Why were all those men out here where there was so much *nothing?* She didn't like this; she didn't like it at all. The hairs on the back of her neck stood up. "Jim, just back up," she commanded. Men usually listened intently to her commands, but not dim Jim.

"I'll ask for directions this time. Guess I should've done that at the gas station we passed."

"Guess so," Jayne muttered, fingering her pearls almost furiously.

Jim pulled the Mercedes to a slow gentle stop in the middle of the road. He grabbed his keys, turned on the small flashlight that hung from his keychain and gave her a dazzling smile. "I'll be right back."

Just a few feet away, the six men huddled around the trunk of one car watched Jim step from the Mercedes. Jayne knew she was a bit of a snob; her mother had trained her well. But even if she hadn't been such a self-confessed elitist, she would've felt uneasy at the sight of these six men.

All of them were dressed in jeans and T-shirts, and at first glance it seemed they all fingered or puffed on cigarettes. In this day and age, who smoked? One of the men had long greasy hair. The fidgeting kid beside him had either very short hair or none at all. The light was not good enough for her to be certain. The unusually tall man who stood beside the open trunk of one of the cars was so large that his rounded belly, tightly encased in a ripped Harley-Davidson T-shirt, hung in a distressing way over his low-slung jeans. Two of the men were more conservative in appearance than the others, looking almost out of place. Their jeans were pressed, their T-shirts were free of wrinkles and tucked into those jeans, and each of them had what could only be described as an executive haircut. They stood side by side, obviously together. The sixth man…the sixth man hung back a little, his face in shadow. But he looked as common as the others in tight jeans and heavy boots and a leather jacket. A leather jacket, at this time of year? The nights could become cool here, she knew, but late spring was definitely not the proper season for leather. Grandmother would call them all hooligans.

Jim shone his flashlight before him, checking the road for potholes as he called out a cheerful greeting. "Hi, fellas. I seem to have gotten myself lost..."

Jayne heard nothing more except a loud popping noise that made her jump. Jim crumpled to the ground before her eyes and disappeared from her limited view. She snapped her eyes to the crowd of thugs. The two more conservatively dressed men backed warily away from the others. The man with the long greasy hair calmly lit another cigarette and offered the pack to his bald friend.

The large man who had done the shooting waved the gun in his hand toward the thug in the leather jacket, who seemed to be arguing with him.

It took a moment for the information to register, for her heart to quit beating so fast that she couldn't even think. They'd shot Jim. *Shot* him. Poor dumb Jim, whose only crime was getting lost on the way to Marsh's vacation home, who was the worst blind date Jayne had ever suffered...who had taken the keys to the car with him.

The greasy-haired hood spoke softly and nodded toward the car, and the bald one headed her way. She had nowhere to run to, and even if she did, she wasn't likely to get far in the high heels that matched her chic coral suit. She thought of kicking off her shoes and running in her bare feet, but she knew how rocky the land she'd have to run across would be. Her feet needed to be protected. She wasn't going anywhere fast. Still, if she could manage to get lost in the darkness...

Before the hoodlum reached the car, Jayne threw open the passenger door and sprinted out. She ran without looking back, her legs a little wobbly on the uncertain terrain, thanks to her high heels. She was supposed to be at a political party, sipping wine and drumming up support for her father, not running from a murder!

The men behind her seemed to all shout at once, as Jayne ran farther and farther into the darkness. She didn't know where she was headed, but she didn't care as long as that place was away from the scene of the shooting. Behind her the gun fired again, and she actually heard the bullet zing past her ear. A man shouted, another yelled, a third howled like a wolf, and still Jayne ran without looking back. A car engine roared. She could hope that they would all leave, couldn't she? They could take off, leaving her to disappear into the darkness.

No such luck. Long before she heard the heavy footfall behind her, she knew that running from the hoodlums was a hopeless cause. If they wanted to catch her, if they wanted to stop her, they could. Several of them were chasing her, or so it seemed from the sound of the approaching steps and the vile curses she heard muttered and shouted. A harsh voice ordered her to stop.

Her heart pounded so hard she thought it would burst through her chest. She couldn't breathe, and her legs ached. Every step was perilous in the heels. But she was *not* going to stop.

Without further warning she was caught from behind. Arms snaked around her waist, snared her, held her, and with those arms on and all around her, she fell to the ground. She screamed breathlessly, and the man who'd caught her let out a loud *whoosh* as he landed practically on top of her. Since his arms were already completely around her, she was partially protected from her fall to the hard-packed ground. But still, it *hurt*.

Jayne closed her eyes, lost in darkness and the weight and suffocating heat of the man lying atop her. They were going to kill her, just like they'd killed poor Jim. Dammit, she would never forgive Pamela for this.

"On your feet, sugar," the one who had caught her ordered.

He dragged her up, keeping his hand tightly around her wrist even when they were standing face-to-face. Well, her face to his broad chest was more like it. It was the hoodlum in the leather jacket who had caught her, and he wasn't even breathing hard! She could barely catch her breath.

The man who had shot Jim raised his weapon and pointed it at her. Jayne closed her eyes.

"Put that down," the man in the leather jacket ordered calmly. He took a step to the side, effectively shielding her. "Does she look like a fed? Does she look like some dealer who's here to snatch your stuff? Hell, what we have here are two yuppies who have the misfortune to be in the wrong place at the wrong time." He turned to face her again, and she had no choice but to see his stubbled jaw and cruel lips. And though she couldn't see well in the dark, she sensed that the look in his eyes was accusing, as if this catastrophe was all her fault.

"Don't matter," the fat man with the gun in his hand said. "She's seen us. Ain't nothing else I can do but shoot her." He sounded so matter-of-fact, so insanely logical.

The man who held her too tightly shook his head in what appeared to be dismay. His long dark hair swayed softly, his stubbled jaw clenched. And he muttered the most foul of words beneath his breath. The grip on her wrist was a vise she didn't even try to fight. He jerked her around thoughtlessly, placing his body between her and the man with the gun. All the while he cursed, low and gruff. His body tensed; a muscle in his jaw twitched.

"I want her," he growled.

The fat man lowered his gun. "You what?"

"I said I want her," he repeated in an almost grudging manner. "We've been stuck out at that damn shack for over a month, and let me tell you, the women in that pisshole you call a town aren't exactly up to my standards."

Jayne panicked all over. "I'd rather die," she said. She tried to jerk away from the man and attempted to kick him where it was supposed to hurt the most. She ended up falling, landing on her backside in the dirt. The grip on her wrist never let up.

The man who manacled her wrist turned his shadowed face toward her, leaned down and whispered, "Be careful what you wish for, sugar."

Boone kept his body between the woman and the gun. She thanked him by kicking him in the knee with a pointy-toed shoe. He had a feeling she'd been aiming higher before she'd lost her balance and stumbled. The skirt of her obviously expensive suit rode high on her shapely thighs. Her knees knocked together and her toes pointed in, in a fashion that should have been comical but wasn't.

Light from Marty's wavering flashlight raked over the woman's body. Soft, barely curling hair not much longer than chin-length brushed pale cheeks. That baby-fine hair was blond, he thought, but not golden. A touch of red made it brighter. Different. The pearls she wore around her neck were surely real and expensive, like everything else about her. Her suit was the color of an Easter egg, not pink and not orange, not pale and not bright. She was all creamy white and golden pink, and she was rightfully frightened half out of her mind.

Focusing on her gave him a moment to collect his thoughts, to still his racing heart. No one was supposed to die here. Tonight's sale was to have been a simple exchange, a little business Darryl had to take care of before his next meeting with the man who ran things around here. Boone had had no choice but to tag along, taking mental notes, knowing that in less than a week this entire operation would be shut down. Just a few more days, and he'd be meeting the infamous Joaquin Gurza face-to-face.

"Watch your step, sugar," he said as he hauled the woman to her feet.

"Do not call me sugar, you…you goon," she said indignantly. Her honeyed Southern drawl reminded him of home.

He cast a glance at Darryl, the drug dealer who'd been so quick to pull his gun and fire. Boone cursed himself for not seeing it coming. He likely couldn't do a damn thing about the man lying in the road, but he'd do his best to save the woman—if she'd let him.

"Well, then, what's your name, darlin'?"

She hit him, hauling off and landing a pathetic punch on his upper arm. "My name is none of your business," she snapped.

Darryl laughed. "Come on, Becker," he said. "Have at her and then let me shoot her. She looks like an awful lot of trouble, and she's got a big mouth."

Boone placed his face close to the woman's. "Sugar, your choices are limited," he whispered. "You shut your mouth and stick close to me, or you end up like

the man in the road.'' Even in the dark he could see the
new wave of panic that flitted across her pretty face.
''Was he your husband?''

She shook her head.

''Boyfriend?''

She shook her head again.

He couldn't afford to tell her too much, but he sure
as hell couldn't hand her over to Darryl. Marty and
Doug, who looked on as if this was the most amusing
scene they'd witnessed in a long while, weren't much
better. Nope, the woman was his responsibility—until
he figured out how to get rid of her.

''No,'' he said, his eyes on the woman, his words for
Darryl. ''I'm not going to 'have at her' and you're not
going to shoot her. It's not going to be that easy.''

The woman's lips trembled, and she lowered her
eyes. Maybe she didn't want him to see the fear that
had to be there. Oh, God, he hoped she didn't start to
cry. He had no patience with weepy women.

''I'm taking her with me.'' With that, he turned and
headed back toward the car.

Darryl didn't like the idea of taking the woman along,
but he simply grumbled a curse and stuck his pistol into
his waistband.

The buyers were long gone, having collected their
purchase and taken off as Boone and the others chased
the witness. They'd wisely left the money, neatly bound
and stacked in a small suitcase, sitting in the trunk of
Darryl's car.

Boone sped up and headed toward the man on the
ground. He moved so fast the woman he dragged behind
him had to run to keep up. Every foul word he'd ever
used came to mind. He muttered them all.

''You have a vulgar mouth,'' the woman said primly,
keeping her voice low.

"Yep."

"A gentleman would never use such language in front of a lady."

Boone stopped and stared down at the man who was sprawled on the ground by the Mercedes, taking everything in quickly. High-priced suit, gold watch, salon haircut. A perfect match for the woman at his side. He hated people like these. Holier than thou, too rich for their own good, always looking down their noses at the rest of the world. They didn't deserve to get shot for it, though.

He didn't have much time. Keeping a firm grip on the woman's wrist, he dropped to his haunches and quickly rifled through the man's pockets.

"What are you doin'?" Marty called.

Boone glanced over his shoulder. The kid who combed his hair with a razor was heading right for him.

"Checking the man's pockets. He looks like he has money, doesn't he?" With that Boone ripped off the watch and stuck it in his pocket.

The woman made a sound that was a tsk and a sigh and a grunt rolled into one feminine utterance, revealing her utter disgust with him.

Marty grinned. "Can I have the car?"

"No," Boone said tersely. "It'll lead the cops right to us."

Doug came up behind his buddy. As the woman's frightened eyes landed on him, Doug flipped his long hair like a vain woman trolling in a bar. "And she won't?" he asked bitterly.

"I'll take care of her," Boone promised darkly.

Doug and Marty were not much older than twenty, neither was too bright, and they scared easily. All those facts had made Boone's time here much easier than it might have been.

Still, no matter how dumb they were, he couldn't finish what he had to do with them looking on. "Put the girl in Darryl's car," he said, offering her imprisoned arm to Marty. Just before Marty grabbed the woman's wrist, he felt a deep tremble pass through her body. *Sorry, sugar,* he thought silently. *I have no choice.* "Touch her anywhere else," he added darkly, "and I'll kill you. She's mine." Marty's grin faded rapidly, and Boone said, "I'll be right there."

Doug and Marty moved away, Marty with his hand gripping the woman's arm, Doug quickly checking the front seat of the Mercedes. Darryl was occupied getting his money situated, which gave Boone the opportunity to place his fingers against the neck of the man on the ground.

He closed his eyes in relief. The man wasn't dead. His heartbeat was strong and steady. What happened next was necessarily fast. Boone found the wound on the man's side. It was nasty, but not fatal. He prayed the guy didn't come to and start making noise. Darryl would finish the job if that happened.

Moving quickly, Boone removed the man's jacket. In the process, he snagged the wallet—in case anyone was watching. The cell phone in the inside pocket dropped into his hand.

The jacket made an easy, quick, inadequate bandage. But it was better than nothing. Keeping his hands out of sight, Boone switched on the cell phone and dialed 911. He positioned the phone on the man's chest, then concealed the phone with a flapping portion of the fancy jacket that he had fashioned into a bandage.

"Come on!" Darryl shouted, slamming the trunk of his car closed and heading for the driver's-side door. Marty and Doug were already sitting in the back seat, the terrified hostage pinned between them.

There was no more time. If Darryl decided to come over and see what he was doing, the operation was finished. Done. Three months' work wasted and someone dead. Either Darryl, or Boone himself and the woman.

Boone leaned forward and whispered, giving the 911 operator who had answered the emergency call the name of the road they were on. Nothing more. It would take them a while to find the exact location, but the delay couldn't be helped. At least the man on the ground had a strong pulse and wasn't bleeding too seriously.

"Hang in there, buddy," he whispered.

He couldn't afford to be caught. Not tonight. He hadn't yet found the child the drug dealer Gurza had kidnapped, and until he did, nothing else mattered. Not this man and not the woman.

He shook his head as he strode away from the Mercedes and the man on the ground. Very faintly, he heard the tinny sound of the operator's voice from the cell phone asking for more information.

What a night. A man shot, a hostage he was now responsible for…he was in too deep. Things were going very wrong, and once things started going wrong, they usually didn't stop. They just got worse.

There was going to be hell to pay, but not until he found that kid and delivered him home.

Chapter 2

Jayne shook. She didn't want the murdering kidnappers to know how scared she was, but no matter how she tried to stop the all-over shaking, it continued.

The two men who bracketed her stared straight ahead and didn't acknowledge her presence at all, even though the three of them sat thigh to thigh in the rear seat of the dark sedan. They were obviously afraid of the one they called Becker, who kept casting dark warning glances into the back seat.

She might have been protected from the seedier side of life since birth and she was definitely frightened now, but Jayne had enough wits about her to be very well aware of what had happened. She and Jim had happened upon a drug deal. Just their luck. Of all the roads to get lost on, Jim had chosen *that* one. She sniffled, just a little, and fingered her pearls. Jim was dead, and she soon would be. Unless she found a way to escape.

Becker glanced into the back seat again, his eyes

landing on hers briefly as they passed under a street
lamp. Her mouth went dry. Her heart thundered. It took
no imagination at all to realize what *he* wanted from
her. He'd told his friends plainly enough. Her shaking
got worse.

For a split second she thought she saw those dark
eyes soften, and then they passed out of the light and
his face was lost in darkness again. She shook her head.
Any hint of softness she saw in that man was a hopeful
illusion.

The car came to a stop in front of a ramshackle house
in the middle of nowhere. A single low-wattage lightbulb glowed near the front door, lighting the less-than-
illustrious dwelling too well. The gray paint on the
walls was peeling, and the windows she could see had
been covered in bedsheets, instead of curtains. There
were no neighbors, but for the similar shack they had
passed a mile or so back. And in truth, it had looked
deserted.

She should be sipping wine at Corbin Marsh's extravagant Arizona vacation home. Instead, she was…
here.

By the time the bald thug exited the car, Becker was
waiting for her. He looked none too happy as he offered
his hand. Jayne refused to touch that hand as she
stepped from the car. There was nowhere to go and she
already knew she couldn't run fast enough. Still, she
glanced toward the gravel road.

"Don't even think about it," Becker said softly as
he took her arm. "You wouldn't get far."

Because he'd shoot her? Because one of the other
hoodlums would?

Jayne gathered every ounce of strength she had left
and looked him in the eye. "Bully," she said.

The other three laughed, but not Becker. The fat man who had shot poor Jim slapped his long-haired friend on the back. "I shoot her boyfriend, and you drag her back here to have your way with her, and the worst she can come up with is 'bully'?" He snorted like a pig.

Jayne was tempted to look the fat man in the eye and deliver a criticism in his direction...but she didn't. Becker scared her, but the man who had shot Jim and threatened to do the same to her terrified her beyond reason. She sensed that if she kept her eyes and attention on Becker, she might get through this.

They were all thugs, but the one who had claimed her as his own seemed to be the most intelligent of the four. Maybe when they were alone, she could reason with him. Offer him money to get her out of here, safe and untouched. Her father could and would pay anything to rescue her. Could Becker be bought? And if so, how much would it take?

She was led to a side entrance, where no light burned. As soon as the bald young hooligan threw that door open, she could tell that the interior of the shack was worse than the exterior. She would have thought that impossible. Becker led her through the door and into the kitchen. Fast-food bags and beer cans littered the floor, and the counter and sink were stacked high with dirty dishes. She had to step over a discarded pizza box as Becker dragged her through.

"Hey," one of the younger criminals said as he followed them in. Jayne looked over her shoulder and saw it was the kid with the long greasy hair. "I wouldn't step on your toes or anything," he continued, grinning at Becker. "But maybe when you're through with her, the bitch could clean this place up a bit."

Jayne's eyes shot fire at the kid.

"Clean it up yourself, Doug," Becker said without looking back.

Doug's smile died quickly, and he scowled at Becker's back.

The living area was no better than the kitchen. More fast-food wrappings and beer cans littered the place, appropriate accompaniment to newspapers, a canted couch and a couple of chairs that looked as if they might have been retrieved from a trash pile. A small television sat on a table against one wall. No cable, she noticed, just a rabbit-ear antenna. A new fear gripped her. If they found out who she was, who her *father* was, would they decide to hold her for ransom? Or would they panic and dispose of her as quickly as possible?

Becker led her into a narrow hallway carpeted in faded and stained green. No matter how hard she tried to calm herself, nothing worked. Her heart pounded, her breathing was shallow, her knees shook. She found herself hanging back, fighting against Becker's grip as he opened a door and dragged her into what appeared to be a bedroom. Behind her, she heard the two younger criminals laugh again.

With one last yank, Becker dragged her all the way inside and slammed the door shut. Her first thought was that at least this room was cleaner than the rest of the house. The double bed had been hastily made, there was no garbage on the floor, and the single narrow window was actually covered with a curtain, not a sheet.

"Sit down," Becker ordered softly.

The only place to sit was the bed. Jayne shook her head in silent refusal.

Becker leaned in closer, just a bit. The dark of night had shadowed much of his face, but the uncovered lightbulb that burned overhead illuminated every detail.

Dark-brown eyes that held no laughter. A sharp jaw dusted with dark stubble and softened by the long dark-brown hair that fell over his shoulder. A long, perfectly shaped nose, a wide, perfectly shaped mouth. A big gun shoved almost carelessly into the waistband of his jeans.

"Sit," he whispered.

Jayne sat. She perched on the side of the bed with her hands in her lap, her spine rigid and her knees together. "My father will pay a lot of money to get me back, unhurt and, uh…" She swallowed hard. *Untouched.* She couldn't say that out loud, but surely he knew what she meant.

Becker paced by the side of the bed, staying between her and the door, running his hands through his hair and pushing the long brown strands away from his face. He kept his eyes on the floor, and occasionally he glanced at the door. Only once did he look at her, and when he did he shook his head and groaned low in his throat before casting that dark gaze to the floor again.

Finally he stopped pacing and stood before her. Close. Too close. And she had nowhere to go.

Boone stared at the girl on the bed. What the hell was he going to do with her?

"What's your name?" he asked.

She flinched. "I'm not telling you anything," she said frostily.

He almost smiled. She should be crying, hysterical, terrified, but she still had the guts to look at him coldly. She couldn't hide the way her hands and knees shook, though. "Well, then, I'll just call you sugar."

She pursed her lips. "Jayne," she said.

"No last name?"

"Not that I'd care to share with you."

He leaned forward and down. "Don't play hardball with me, lady. I'm your only chance of getting out of here alive."

She swallowed, sending that slender, pale throat working in interesting ways.

In the hallway someone snickered. Doug or Marty...probably both.

Boone sighed. "Give me your jacket," he ordered.

"I will not."

He slipped off his leather jacket and placed it on the end of the bed, pulled off his T-shirt and tossed it atop the jacket. He drew the Colt pistol from his waistband, looked at the weapon, looked at the woman, then quickly went to the closet and placed the pistol on the top shelf. He didn't think Jayne would actually try to shoot him, but until they got things straightened out here, he couldn't be sure—and she wouldn't be able to reach the top shelf without a ladder or a chair. Neither was handy.

That done, he waggled his fingers at her, silently asking again for the jacket to her expensive suit. She stubbornly lifted her chin and shook her head.

"I'm not going to touch you," he said through clenched teeth. "But I need that damn jacket."

She sniffled and crossed her arms over her chest.

"Fine," he said. "We do this the hard way." He sat beside her and grasped one wrist in his hand. She fought a little, but not very hard.

"Get your hands off of me," she said loudly, slapping at his hands.

In the hallway, another giggle.

Finally, after just a little wrestling, he had the jacket in his hand. He shook his free finger at her. "Now lie down and be still."

"I will not."

Boone closed his eyes and shook his head. "This is not going to work."

"No, it's not," she agreed.

Boone left the bed and went to the door, opening it on two grinning young thugs. "What the hell are you two doing here?" He shook the jacket as he spoke. They looked past him, no doubt to see a red-faced Jayne sitting on the side of the bed, her hair mussed and her blouse halfway untucked.

"There's nothin' else to do around here," Doug said. "Ain't you finished yet?"

"Some of us like to take more than three minutes with a woman, kid. Get lost. If I see either one of you near this door or that window," he said, jerking a thumb over his shoulder, "I'll shoot you."

"Maybe you oughtta tell her that," Marty said with a lift of his chin.

Boone turned around to see that Jayne stood at the window, tugging frantically at the lower frame. He closed the door and leaned against it, watching her with a shake of his head.

"It's painted shut," he informed her.

She gave one last tug and spun to face him, her eyes red and her cheeks flushed. It hit him, for the first time, how very small she was. Not thin, but short—no more than five foot two—and delicately shaped. Beneath the hem of her straight skirt was a pair of nice legs. Up the length of her body she sported easy curves.

"We need to talk," he said softly. "Sit down."

She shook her head.

"Please," he said, calling on every little bit of patience he had left. "Please sit down. I'm not going to hurt you."

"I imagine you think I should be flattered," she said, trying to sound strong and falling far short. "Am I supposed to be grateful?"

"Well, you would be dead right now if not for me. A little gratitude can't be too much to ask," he said in a low voice. His response did nothing to soothe her. She brought a hand to the pearls at her throat, and her breathing changed, became more rapid. He did *not* need her passing out on him! Calming himself, he raised both hands, palms out. "I swear, I'm not going to touch you. You're safe with me. Now sit on the bed."

She moved warily away from the window, and he stepped into her place, making certain the curtains were tightly closed. He didn't need anyone peeking in, and warning or no warning, he wouldn't put anything past Doug and Marty. When he turned around, he saw that Jayne had done as he asked and was perching prettily on the edge of the bed.

"We need to talk," he said, "but first..."

Her eyes grew wide as he stepped around her to the head of the bed, gripping one corner of the headboard in his hand. He sighed tiredly. How to explain? Best just to do what he had to do.

While Jayne sat warily on the side of the mattress, Boone banged the headboard against the wall. Once. Twice. A third time. He waited a moment, then began again, in a steady rhythm this time. Eyes pinned on the woman, he banged the cheap headboard against the wall over and over.

"You could help," he whispered.

She shook her head. "Help with what?"

"Make a little noise. Pretend to be enjoying yourself."

"I will not," she said indignantly.

With his free hand, Boone reached out and grabbed Jayne's wrist. As he'd suspected she would, she squealed. He smiled. "That'll do."

Jayne clamped her mouth shut and pursed her lips. Oh, she was cute when she got mad. Of course, she'd been mad since he'd met her. Mad and scared.

He sped up the rhythm of the headboard banging against the wall. "Do it again," he ordered in a whisper.

"No, I wo—" At an insistent tug that dragged an unwilling Jayne closer to the head of the bed, she squealed once more.

Oh, this was not good. The way he was holding her made her creamy blouse hug her breasts. She was breathing hard, the way she might if this was not pretend. Her fiery green eyes were latched onto his. And the banging of the headboard reminded him of what he was pretending to do. The rhythm, the shaking of the bed... "One more time, sugar."

"Don't call me—"

He hauled her off the bed so that she came to her feet and ran smack-dab into his bare chest. This time she screamed. Boone whacked the headboard against the wall three more times for good measure, and then he quit.

Jayne glanced up at him, suspicious and still frightened. But then, they hadn't had their little talk yet, so she was less than fully informed.

"Was it good for you?" he whispered.

In answer she slapped him across the cheek, hard and solid.

Jayne realized, as the sound of the slap reverberated in the air, that she should not have hit him. Still, she wasn't sorry.

He laid a big hand over the red mark she'd made on his face. "Sit," he said.

She did, and again he paced in front of her. She wasn't as afraid as she had been. He had only pretended to...well, he'd pretended, and he said they needed to talk. About what? Ah, likely he was interested in her offer of money from her father.

"My daddy will pay you anything..."

"Let's leave your daddy out of this, shall we?" Becker said testily. "I'm trying to figure things out."

"Figure what out?"

"What to do with you, sugar."

Jayne bit her lower lip. There were worse things to be called than sugar, she supposed.

Finally Becker stopped pacing and stood before her, bare-chested, bigger than most men, all muscle and hair and tight jeans and penetrating eyes. There was something intimidating about him. Something intense. Of course he was intimidating!

"Can I trust you?" he asked, the question seeming to be more for himself than for her. "God, what a mess." He then began to mumble a string of profanity that had Jayne blushing.

"Do you mind?" she finally asked.

"Do I mind what?"

"Don't curse."

He actually grinned. "We are in so much trouble I can't see a way out, and you're worried about my language?"

"There's no reason to be crude."

"Sugar, crude is my middle name."

Jayne wrinkled her nose. "That doesn't surprise me."

Becker sat beside her, and Jayne scooted away. But she didn't jump up, which had been her first instinct. If he had planned to hurt her, he would have done so by now. Still, she felt too small sitting next to him, and a little distance wouldn't hurt.

Voice lowered, Becker leaned close. "I'm here undercover."

A surge of relief washed through her. "Oh, thank God. DEA? FBI? You must have some way to call in backup or something, right? There are probably a bunch of agents out there in the dark, waiting for your signal so they can storm the house. Right?"

He laid dark eyes on her and sighed. "No backup. I'm a private investigator, and I'm here on my own."

Her relief was short-lived. "No backup?"

He shook his head.

Jayne was determined to make the best of the situation. "But you're not one of *them*, not a...a bad guy, and you can get me out of here, right?"

"Eventually."

"What do you mean, eventually? Those men killed Jim, and they almost killed me—"

"Your friend's not dead," Becker interrupted. "He'll be fine. You'll be fine. But I need a few more days."

She shook her head. "But—"

"I'm not going to blow three months of work just to get your pretty little ass out of here."

"But—"

"Don't ask me to throw away everything I've done to this point because you were foolish or unlucky enough to stumble onto Darryl's drug deal."

"Can't you sneak me out of here and make it look like I escaped?"

Becker shook his head. "I don't think so. Darryl would come after you for sure. If I keep you close, if we…make them think you don't mind being close, I think I can keep you alive until I'm done here."

"You *think?* How comforting."

"It's the best I've got right now."

She studied his face for a moment, the lines and the tense set of his jaw. Should she tell him who her father was? Maybe not. Wouldn't make any difference, and he might think she was trying to use the family name to get him to change his plan and get her out of here tonight, his three months' work unimportant in the light of her father's public and political stature.

"Is Becker your real name?"

He shook his head.

"Are you going to tell me your real name?"

He sighed. "Boone, but don't use it outside this room. For the duration, I'm Richard Becker."

"Is Boone your first name or your last?"

"Does it matter?"

Jayne sighed. She could feel her body relaxing, unwinding, ratcheting down. She'd survived. With this man's help she'd continue to survive. "I'd like to know."

"Boone Sinclair, private investigator, ma'am." He offered his hand.

Jayne cautiously took it. "Jayne Barrington."

The threat momentarily gone, Jayne saw Boone in a whole new light. The strength that had been menacing became consoling. His dark good looks were suddenly interesting, rather than intimidating. They shook hands briefly, Boone's big hand gentle around hers, the contact unexpectedly comforting.

"Jim's really not dead?"

Boone shook his head. "Darryl winged him. He's lost some blood." A smile flitted across a hard face. "I think your friend fainted."

A shiver worked down Jayne's spine. "I thought he was dead."

"Don't worry," Boone growled. "You'll be out of here and comforting him in no time."

She shook her head. "No. In truth, I barely know Jim." She settled her eyes on his, dark and deep and unreadable. "Blind date."

"How did you end up on Springer Road?"

"We were on our way to a party and got lost." She couldn't believe her luck. If Boone Sinclair hadn't been there, if he hadn't rescued her, she'd be dead now. Her grandmother would say that Boone was an angel sent to save her. That it had been no accident that he'd been there, working undercover. She smiled.

"What are you grinning about?" He dipped his head and looked into her eyes. "You're not going to lose it on me, are you?"

Jayne shook her head. "No. It's just that…you don't look at all like an angel."

"Trust me," he said in a low voice. "I'm not."

She tried not to stare at his bare chest. He didn't seem to mind at all sitting here, half-naked, broader and more muscled than an ordinary man. "What are you doing here? I didn't know private investigators could do undercover work."

That got a half grin out of him. "I didn't say it was legal."

Jayne pursed her lips slightly. As a politician's

daughter, she'd lived all her life under a microscope.
Every detail, every decision, every move properly scru-
tinized. She couldn't even leave the house without carefully checking her clothes, makeup and hair. To disre-
gard the law with a smile...she couldn't even imagine.

Boone frowned. "I see you don't approve."

"It's just...I'm sure you have your reasons." In
truth, she didn't care why he was here. Just that he was.

"I do."

Jayne sighed. Boone had been honest with her. It was
the least she could do for him.

"My father—"

"Can't we leave Daddy out of this?" Boone said
again.

Jayne looked him in the eye. "I don't think so." He
waited for her to continue. Eyes steady, chest bare, dark
hair hanging over his shoulders. "My father is a United
States senator. From Mississippi," she added. "Augus-
tus Barrington."

He remained silent.

"Jim and I were on our way to a party given by a
potential supporter who might go a long way in aiding
my father financially should he decide to run for...a
higher office."

Boone didn't so much as move. Did he even breathe?

"My disappearance is going to cause an uproar," she
went on. "A big one. My father will do his best to get
every government agency available on the job. So we
have until morning. Maybe."

Boone ran one hand through his hair and let loose
with an even viler string of profanity than before. He
didn't look at her, but stared at the floor and the wall
and the window as he cursed.

"Mr. Sinclair," she chided softly, censure in her soft voice, "do you mind?"

He fixed his gaze on her again and responded succinctly with the most foul of forbidden words.

Jayne tightened her lips. "You know, there are other words you can call upon when you're upset."

"Really," he drawled.

"Darn or drat or a good doggone work just as well."

He grinned at her, insolent and amused. And again muttered what seemed to be his favorite word.

"Or fudge," she said lightly. "I have, on frustrating occasions when no one is about, muttered an 'oh, fudge' myself."

"Oh, fudge," he growled.

"See?" She smiled. If nothing else, she did know how to get men to do as she wished. It was a gift. "That works just fine, doesn't it?"

Boone left the bed quickly, his back to her as he retrieved his T-shirt. Good! He was going to get dressed. As fine a specimen as he was, his bare chest had become quite distracting.

"Here," he said, turning and tossing the garment to her. "Put this on."

Jayne caught the shirt, then held it cautiously between two fingers. "I'm perfectly comfortable in my own clothes, thank you. Besides—" she sniffed "—you've worn this, and it hasn't been washed."

Boone pressed the bridge of his nose between two fingers, as if he had a headache coming on. "In less than a week I should be done here. Three months of work, down to a matter of days, and now this. I can keep you alive, but you have to listen to me. You have to let me do what I do best."

"What's that?" Jayne whispered.

"Lie." He dropped his hand and glared at her. "As far as Darryl and those two idiots of his are concerned, you and I are hot and heavy."

"Hot and heavy?" She took an unsteady breath. "You just...you dragged me away from the car back there...and you *kidnapped* me. What kind of woman would willingly become intimately involved with a man who literally dragged her to his...his cave as if she were nothing more than..."

Boone's raised hand silenced her. "I know," he said. "But we're looking for two things here. One, we want to keep them away from you."

Jayne shuddered.

"You wear my clothes, you stick close to me at all times, we spend a lot of time right here in this bed." He took an unsteady breath of his own. "You're *mine*. We make it clear that you're *mine*. The guys know that if they try anything funny, they'll have me to contend with."

And Boone Sinclair looked as if he would be awe-inspiring to contend with.

"Two, we want to keep you alive."

"Definitely." Jayne nodded emphatically.

"If they think you're going to keep trying to run away, one of them is going to get antsy and...do something drastic."

Kill you. Boone didn't say the words, but Jayne knew what he meant.

"So you stick to me," he said, as if he didn't like the idea at all. "You lie low, keep your mouth shut, and in a few days I deliver you home."

She still didn't know why Boone Sinclair was here. He could get them both out of this horrible place whenever he wanted, she had no doubt of that. So why didn't he? What was so important that he would risk both their lives? "You never did tell me why you're here," she said softly.

"No, I didn't."

"If I'm going to have to...pretend to like you and all that, shouldn't I know?"

He pinned his eyes to hers again. Oh, he had a way of looking at her that made her arms tingle and her toes curl. She unconsciously raised her arms to hug herself, to chase away the unexpected chill.

"No," Boone finally said, and then he left the room, slamming the door behind him.

Chapter 3

A night of sleeping on the hard floor did nothing to improve Boone's disposition. He had planned to ask Jayne if she minded sharing the bed—platonically, of course—but she'd been sound asleep by the time he'd returned to the room last night. Asleep! She either trusted him completely, a frightening possibility, or she had no self-preservation instincts whatsoever. Neither option was good.

If she'd come awake in the middle of the night and found him sleeping beside her, she probably would have come off the bed screaming. Which wouldn't have necessarily been a bad thing, now that he thought about it. The occasional cry in the night was probably expected.

He rolled up and peered over the edge of the mattress to find Jayne still sleeping. She hadn't put on his T-shirt as he'd told her to. She slept in a silky white slip. He hadn't known women still wore slips! All he could see of the undergarment were the straps, one of which had fallen off her shoulder, but last night he'd caught a glimpse of white against the thigh that had escaped from beneath the sheet on his bed. He'd covered that thigh, feeling a little guilty for enjoying the sight so much, and Jayne hadn't tossed the covers off in the night. If anything, she caught the covers to her more tightly and securely than she had last night, hiding there beneath white sheets and the twisted green comforter.

As he watched, her eyes fluttered, opened, latched onto his and went wide with terror.

Jayne Barrington, demure Southern belle and his unwilling hostage, sat up, bringing the sheet with her. "Oh, no, it wasn't a nightmare," she said breathlessly. "You're…you're real."

"Not the response I usually elicit from women I spend the night with," Boone grumbled.

She took in the makeshift pallet on the floor, and her frightened expression softened. "You could have slept on the couch in the other room."

"You could have left room for me on the bed, so I wouldn't have to sleep on the…darn floor."

Her lip actually curled. "I don't think so."

Annoying as she was, the girl recovered quickly. "So, what's next?"

"Make me breakfast?"

She looked as horrified as she had at the prospect of sleeping with him. "I don't cook!"

"Of course you don't," he muttered, coming to his feet.

She quickly covered her eyes. "You're naked!"

"I am not!" Boone glanced down at the underwear he wore, a pair of baggy silk boxers that were, by his standards, modest.

She did not drop the hand from her eyes, protecting

herself from the sight of his scantily clad body as she continued in a much calmer voice. "*Nearly* naked. Don't you have a pair of pajamas?"

Boone stared at her and shook his head. "No."

"Maybe you could get some."

He laughed at the absurdity of the suggestion. "I don't think so."

Jayne sighed and finally lowered her hand, but she didn't look at him. Her eyes were turned to the window and the morning light that broke through the sliver of a part in the curtains.

Boone heard a footfall in the hallway outside the bedroom door. When he raised a finger to his lips, Jayne nodded her head and pursed her lips. She was spoiled and rich, a debutante who had no business here, but she was quick, he'd give her that.

He grabbed the corner post of the headboard.

"Not again," Jayne whispered.

Boone shrugged and began to rock. Jayne lay down on the bed and covered her face with the sheet, squealing softly but appropriately when he reached down to pinch her lightly on one gently curving, sheet-covered shoulder.

Jayne had brushed off Boone's suggestion that she wear one of his T-shirts and cinch up an old pair of cutoff denims, and dressed in her own clothes. Blouse and skirt, anyway, and shoes. No hose, no jacket, but she had retrieved her pearls from the bedside table and put them on, and she'd brushed her hair. Fortunately one of the hooligans had collected her purse from the Mercedes. Her cell phone was gone, of course, but she had her own brush, as well as a small amount of makeup. *Very* fortunately the criminal who had reached into the car for her purse hoping for a nice wad of cash hadn't recognized the name Barrington on her driver's license, a name her father had made well-known. In truth, she had done nothing on her own accord but to uphold the family name and play hostess for the sociable Senator Barrington when he asked it of her.

She plopped a large plate of bacon and eggs on the kitchen table, and the four men present stared suspiciously at the offering.

"The bacon's not done," Marty grumbled.

Doug picked up the strip nearest him, an almost black piece of bacon that had gotten away from her and turned dark before her very eyes. "This one is."

"Bacon's not good for you, anyway," Boone said as he reached for the spoon Jayne had left in the scrambled eggs, took a huge spoonful and dropped it onto his plate.

Darryl grumbled, but he filled his own plate, too, and the four men began to eat. They each took a bite. Three men spit half-chewed eggs back onto their plates.

Boone swallowed, grudgingly. "Sugar, hand me the salt."

"Salt!" Jayne said, turning around and heading for the kitchen counter. "I forgot all about the salt."

"We figured that out for ourselves," Doug said under his breath.

"There's no need to be rude," Jayne said as she placed the saltshaker on the table, directly in front of Boone. "I'm not a cook, you know. If you don't like what I made for breakfast, you can just quietly walk away and either go hungry or make your own breakfast."

Darryl, the man who had shot Jim, narrowed one eye. He still gave Jayne a major case of the shivers. She didn't think it was simply his large size that frightened her. He'd shot and intended to kill Jim; he would have shot her without a second thought, without a twinge of conscience. Boone she could handle; the boys who giggled like teenage girls when they thought of sex she could handle. But Darryl...Darryl was much too frightening for her to even consider handling.

"If she's going to stay here, she's going to pull her weight," Darryl said.

"She will," Boone replied. Without warning, he grabbed her and pulled her onto his knee. "She *does*," he added suggestively.

Jayne tried to stand; Boone held her in place. She knew what he was doing and she knew why. That didn't mean she had to *like* it. "Not now," she chided. "I have dishes to do. The kitchen is a mess." She tried again to stand, and got only a few inches off his knee before he pulled her down again. She landed with a thump on his rock-hard thigh.

"I didn't bring you here to do dishes," he said in a voice low enough to be meant for her alone, loud enough to carry to the other three, who ate newly salted eggs and picked at their bacon looking for properly cooked segments. "Doug and Marty can do the damned dishes."

"Don't curse," she said primly.

Boone tightened the arm that encircled her waist and pulled her back. "Don't tell me what to do." With that, he nudged aside her hair and pressed his lips to her neck. She couldn't help it; she let out a squeaky breathless cry.

Doug giggled. "She is a squealer, ain't she, Becker. Doesn't that get on your nerves? All that howling?"

"No," Boone responded, his mouth still against her neck.

"I really should do the..." Something wet trailed across the back of her neck. His mouth...his *tongue.* "Dishes."

Jayne wasn't tough, she wasn't prepared for a situation like this one, and yet at the moment she felt as if she had absolutely no control. None. The world was spinning, she didn't know what would happen next...and she was just along for the ride. She hated that, rolling along with no say in the matter, a man's hands on her body and his mouth on her neck giving her inappropriate and unexpected and *unwanted* chills. Another man watched, ready to kill her at the slightest provocation. Two other brainless hoodlums looked on, amused.

Boone said that what he did best was lie. It was a game. A deadly one, but a game all the same. If she was to play, perhaps she could gather her wits and *play.* What would it take to garner a bit of control? Some semblance of order?

She grasped Boone's wrist and forcefully moved it aside. She stood, removing her neck from his lascivious attentions. When he reached out, she very deftly moved out of his way.

"For goodness' sake," Jayne said as she took a step that carried her just out of his reach. "You are incorrigible." They were supposed to be intimate, and while she knew very little about intimacy, she did know that the woman in such a relationship possessed a power of her own. "All night," she said, turning to face Boone as she backed toward the sinkful of dirty dishes. "*And* into the morning. What do you think I am? A...a..." She didn't have to work hard to manufacture a sniffle.

"You should be able to keep your hands to yourself for five minutes. *Five minutes!* Is that too much to ask?"

Boone lifted two finely shaped dark eyebrows. "You didn't complain last night."

"I did!" she said indignantly. Then she remembered his words, what it would take to keep her alive, and she blushed. "At first."

"This is better than a soap opera," Doug said with a grin.

"Do the dishes," Boone finally said, his voice low and his eyes dark.

"You do the dishes!"

"I thought you *wanted* to do the dishes!" Boone sounded truly frustrated.

"God, now they sound like my parents," Marty said with a shudder, pushing away from the table.

Darryl slowly rose to his feet, shook his head, clenched and unclenched his meaty fists. Doug popped up, too, not wanting to be left behind.

Marty, still shaking his head, left the kitchen and headed straight for the television in the connecting living room. "Hey, maybe the news about that guy Darryl shot will be on TV!" Darryl and Doug followed.

The expression on Boone's face changed subtly, darkening. "You missed the morning news."

"Yeah, but the one station we get kinda clear has an update at ten." He glanced at his watch. "Just a couple of minutes."

With his hands positioned so that no one else could see, Boone motioned to Jayne. She had no idea what he was trying to tell her, but she did know one thing: they didn't want these guys to know that Jim was alive or that she was a senator's daughter.

"Don't look at me like that," he said sharply. "You

think what happened last night will keep you alive? Piss
me off and you're history, just like your boyfriend."

Sure enough, a curious Marty glanced into the
kitchen. Doug wasn't far behind. Darryl remained
firmly planted in front of the old television, waiting for
the update.

"You wouldn't dare," she said frostily. "Not after…
you know."

"Sex," Boone said. "You can't even say it!" He
launched into a tirade, using every foul word she had
ever heard and some she hadn't.

"You…you crude bully."

As it had last night, the word *bully* made Darryl
laugh. But he didn't move away from the TV.

"I can be cruder and I can be meaner," Boone promised.

"Impossible."

The teaser about the news update came on, sending
a shiver down Jayne's spine. They had a minute, maybe
less.

Boone crossed the room and swept Jayne off her feet.
"Fight me," he whispered as he hauled her up and
tossed her over his shoulder.

She did, kicking, beating ineffectually against his
back with her fists as he carried her into the living room.

"Can't you do better than that?" Boone whispered.

She tried, but she wasn't a violent person. As Boone
carried her through the doorway into the main room,
where Darryl sat before the television, she fought as
best she could, feet and hands flailing. "You…you un-
civilized brute!"

"Last night you seemed to like that about me,
sugar."

"Don't call me sugar." She glanced up to see that

the two dim-witted criminals grinned, while a disgusted Darryl shook his head in wonder or dismay. Maybe both.

"I'll call you whatever I want to call you." Boone put Jayne on her feet between Darryl and the TV, raising his voice. "Don't forget who you are, or how you got here, or that I might get tired of you at any moment and then you'll be in a world of trouble."

Jayne placed her hands on her hips. "You wouldn't dare! Not after…not after…" She stopped and gave Boone an exasperated huff. Darryl leaned to one side as the newsbreak came on. With an outraged cry, Jayne turned and gave the television a shove. It wobbled backward, finally falling from the unsteady stand and crashing to the floor with a spark and a puff of smoke. The screen went black.

"I can't believe you'd say that to me, not after last night. You said…you said…"

The three other men gathered around the remains of the television as Boone grabbed Jayne and pulled her against his chest. "Now, sugar," he said in a soothing voice, "don't get all upset."

Jayne hid her face against Boone's chest. Oh, Darryl would be furious, but what else could she have done? Pushing the TV off its stand had seemed like a good idea at the time. Now she wondered.

"Becker," Darryl said slowly, "your woman just broke my TV."

"I'll buy you a new TV. That one was a piece of crap, anyway." Boone's arms protected her as he brushed off Darryl's complaint.

"How am I supposed to watch my soaps?" Marty asked, not quite as outraged as Darryl, but definitely unhappy.

"Soaps are for old women," Boone growled. "You'll survive a few days with no TV."

Jayne chanced a quick glance at the three men. None of them were happy with her at the moment. She'd made a lousy breakfast *and* broken their television. "I'm sorry," she said softly. "I just got so upset…" The tremble in her voice was not manufactured; it was very real. She returned her gaze to Boone. "You can be so mean."

He lifted her off her feet and spun her around. "I know how to make you feel better."

"Now?"

"Now."

"But, Boo…"

He shut her up by laying his mouth over hers. Immediately she knew why, and even though she had insisted on knowing, for a split second she wished Boone had never told her his real name. Would she always remember to call him Becker when the others were around? If she forgot in a moment of anger or forgetfulness, it could mean death for both of them.

It wasn't a real kiss, but a necessary caution. Still, his mouth was nice and firm, sweet and gentle. She had a feeling that when Boone really kissed a woman, he did it right.

He took his mouth from hers, a warning gleam in his eyes.

"But, BooBoo," she said when she could speak again, hopefully covering her mistake. "I still haven't done the dishes."

"Marty!" Boone yelled. "Do the damned dishes."

BooBoo! Oh, this was bad. "BooBoo?" he asked, hands on hips as he glared down at Jayne, who sat on the side of the bed looking composed, calm, perfectly in control. One foot rocked, drawing his eye to her shapely ankle.

"It's no worse than sugar."

"Yes," he insisted with a nod of his head, "it is."

He didn't let on that his heart was still hammering. He had thought about shooting the television and then trying to pass it off as a rash moment of rage, but Jayne's seemingly impulsive shove had worked much better. But for how long? They would meet with Gurza in four days. Four days, after three months of undercover work! And one wrong word could blow it in a heartbeat.

"I shouldn't have told you my name," he said in a low voice.

Her face softened. "I know but...I'm glad you did," she whispered. "It makes me feel so much safer."

She wasn't safe, not at all, but he didn't bother to tell her so.

Boone moved to the head of the bed and grasped the post in his hand.

Jayne sighed. "Not again. This is so embarrassing."

Boone ignored her and began to shake the bed. The springs squeaked. Jayne covered her face in her hands.

"Come on, sugar," Boone said softly. "Help me out here."

For a moment she did nothing. Then she dropped her hands from her face, looked him in the eye and gave a little hop that made the bed squeak even more. "Why Becker?" she asked as she gave another little bounce. "Is that like a middle name? A family name?"

Boone leaned down, placing his face close to hers. "Rhymes with my favorite body part," he whispered.

She screwed up her nose. "Becker? Becker doesn't

rhyme with…'' Suddenly her face turned red. "That's disgusting!" she said, her voice rising slightly.

He grinned. "Say that a little bit louder."

"I will not," she said primly.

He began to bang the headboard against the wall, faster and faster, harder and harder. "Moan," he whispered.

"I do not moan," she said, her Southern accent deepening as she protested.

"You poor thing. I guess I'll just have to pinch you again to make you squeal."

"That won't be necessary." She looked away from him, squared her shoulders and took a deep breath. And then she made some kind of noise. It wasn't a moan or a squeal. He wasn't sure exactly what it was.

"If I can barely hear it, *they* can't hear it at all."

She snapped her head around and glared at him. "You know, I'm sure there are women out there who make love silently."

"I've never met one."

"You're vile."

"You're a prude."

It was the wrong, or perhaps the *right* thing to say. *Prude* was an insult Jayne took personally, and her response was apparently going to be to prove him wrong. She closed her eyes, tossed back her head and moaned. The sound was low, long and real enough to make Boone's insides tighten. Her soft voice was the kind that might creep under a man's skin if he went for her type. Which he didn't.

Jayne took a deep breath and moaned again, louder this time. Boone tried to convince himself that Jayne Barrington was not his type *at all*. He liked his women with long dark hair, long legs and plenty up top. Not gentle, delicate curves, but prodigious breasts that made a man's eyes pop out of his head when the woman walked into a room. He shook the bed harder, faster, his eyes on Jayne.

Head back, throat bared, mouth slightly parted, she was a fascinating sight, with her creamy skin and reddish-gold hair and soft lips. Her throat was nice and long, he noticed. Shapely and delicate, like the rest of her. His body began to respond. Enough was enough.

"Scream," he whispered.

She laid those green eyes on him and glared. "Maybe I'm not ready," she mouthed.

He grinned and reached for her with his free hand.

"Okay," she said softly, scooting away from him. She closed her eyes again, took a deep breath and screamed. Loud and long. Boone banged the headboard a couple more times, for good measure and then stopped. Thank God. He really couldn't take much more of this.

"Not bad," he said as he sat beside Jayne on the side of the bed. He took a deep calming breath. "Who were you thinking of when you let loose?"

She looked him in the eye. "Not who, *what.* Snakes."

His eyebrows lifted slightly. "Snakes?"

"I'm terrified of snakes," she said with a shake of her head and a shudder that seemed to rack her from head to toe. "And I don't care if they're poisonous or not. I hate all snakes equally."

"Why?"

Her eyes met his. "I don't have to have a specific reason," she said. "A lot of people hate snakes."

Boone waited a couple of minutes before leaving

Jayne, shaking his head as he stood. It had been a pretty damn good scream.

He wasn't terribly surprised to find a scowling Darryl waiting at the doorway between the hallway and the television-less living room. Marty and Doug were no-where to be seen, but as he glared at Darryl, Boone heard laughter from the kitchen and then a splash of water. The boys were doing the dishes.

"I don't get it," Darryl muttered, his hard eyes on Boone and his arms crossed over his massive chest. "It doesn't make any sense. You hauled that woman here last night because you wanted her in your bed. She was none too happy about the idea at the time, as I remember. And then this morning she's calling you BooBoo and screaming her head off. Something stinks."

Boone grinned. "What can I say? I'm good."

Darryl was not impressed.

Boone's grin faded. "She's a society sweetheart who's been handled with kid gloves all her life. Nobody's ever touched her right, nobody's ever made her scream. Since she's never had one before, she thinks an orgasm means she's in love. Three or four and we're soul mates. Don't worry about Jayne. I can handle her."

"What are you going to do with her when we're through here? I can't have her coming to her senses and talking about what happened last night."

"She won't."

"You can't be sure…"

As far as Darryl knew, Richard Becker was a badass drug dealer from Atlanta, looking to move up a notch in the world. An association with Joaquin Gurza would make that happen. Thanks to big brother Dean—who was a deputy U.S. marshal and had all the right con-nections—and Detective Luther Malone, Boone had the background to make this cover tight. Airtight. Boone would protect Jayne Barrington with his life. Richard Becker wouldn't hesitate to kill anyone who got in his way.

"When I'm finished with Jayne," Boone said tightly, "I'll take care of her. She's the one with the illusions, not me. You have nothing to worry about."

Darryl nodded, slightly mollified. "Glad to hear it."

Boone headed past Darryl, intent on the coffeepot on the kitchen counter. He had to keep Darryl and the boys away from the news for the next four days. Could he do it? If Darryl found out that the man he'd shot was alive and that Jayne was a senator's daughter, he'd panic and insist on doing away with her immediately. And since Boone had told them all that Jayne's friend Jim was dead, Jayne would likely not die alone.

If they got that far, how was he going to get Jayne, the kid and himself out of here alive?

His life and his mission had just become very complicated.

Chapter 4

Jayne lay back in the bed and stared up at the ceiling. A shower had helped her to feel a little better, but still she wished for a change of clothes—her *own* clothes—as well as underwear, a soft nightgown, her hair dryer, and an entire package of chocolate-chip cookies. The soft ones.

She hated being shut up alone in this room, but it was better than facing Darryl and his two brainless accomplices. Even with Boone beside her—and when she left this room, he was always beside her, even going so far as to stand guard at the bathroom door while she showered—she was afraid of those thugs.

Earlier today Darryl had suggested that they turn the doorknob on this bedroom around so that they could lock her in and she couldn't lock her BooBoo out. Boone had hated the idea, and she didn't blame him. If they turned the doorknob around, Darryl would be able to lock them both in if he was of a mind to, and with the window painted shut, they'd be trapped. She had no doubt that Boone could get past the flimsy lock on the door, but reversing the knob would also mean that they couldn't lock the others out at night. That would never do.

Boone had told Darryl that no locked door could keep him out. After that, it hadn't been mentioned again.

Low voices drifted to her from the living room, where the four men had gathered to discuss business. She caught enough words to understand they were talking about drugs, money, some kind of meeting.

She couldn't help but wonder why Boone was here. He wasn't DEA, he wasn't official law enforcement of any kind. So what was he doing here undercover, and what was going to happen in less than a week?

Jayne pulled the comforter to her chin and tried to melt into the mattress. The news of her disappearance had probably reached her parents hours ago. Her mother would be frantic. Lucille Barrington was not a particularly stalwart person, and she had always been a little overprotective of her only child. Her doctor would have given her something to help her rest, Jayne supposed, as he had when Grandpa passed away. Lucille Barrington suffered as a Southern woman should—acutely, and in the privacy of her luxurious bedchamber. Jayne loved her mother dearly, but under certain circumstances the woman could be somewhat melodramatic.

The senator, however, was not a man to sit around and worry, and if any physician had dared to try to give him something to help him rest, he'd probably break the poor man's arm. He had doubtless called in favors, Jayne knew, marshaled the troops, spent the afternoon on the phone shouting and cajoling and doing everything humanly possible to get his daughter home safely.

Grandmother would be praying and cooking. Whenever she got anxious, Myra Jayne Barrington went to the kitchen. During the last senatorial campaign, she'd fed not only her son's entire hometown staff, but a lot of the reporters, as well. By now she was probably feeding the entire town.

Boone said he needed less than a week. She didn't think they had even two days.

When Boone returned, locking the door behind him, Jayne breathed a sigh of relief. She couldn't help it; she felt better when he was near.

He was quieter than usual as he sat on the bed to remove his boots and socks. His clenched jaw did nothing to make her feel safe.

"Do you have a cell phone?" she whispered.

"Yeah," he replied absently.

Thank goodness. "I just know my parents and my grandmother are worried sick."

"Scoot over," Boone said, lying back as if he actually intended to sleep here beside her.

Her first impulse was to give him a gentle shove and refuse to scoot over. But if she was about to ask him for a favor, maybe that wasn't the way to go.

She scooted. "Are you sure this is a good idea?"

"I'm not sleeping on the floor again," he said, stretching out beside her. "I'll stay on top of the covers, you stay beneath." A grin flashed across his face. "That way I can be sure you'll keep your hands to yourself."

Jayne moved to the edge of the bed, giving the big man all the room he might need. "Won't you get... cold?" She had been surprised by the night's chill in this part of the country. Back home, May was warm. Some days felt almost like summer. Here the days were pleasant, but when the sun dropped, it was very clear that winter had not fully departed.

Boone turned his head to look her in the eye. "Are you asking me in?"

Jayne's eyes went wide, and her heart thumped hard. "No! Of course not."

"I didn't think so." He rocked gently and the old bed squeaked.

Not again. "I need to call my mother," Jayne whispered.

"Sorry," Boone said as he rocked again.

"But—"

"We can't take the chance," he said, before she even had a chance to present her argument. He continued to move in a manner that made the bed rock and squeak. "You might be overheard, the call might be traced, and cell phones are notoriously insecure. Besides, my cell company doesn't even have service out here. We'd have to swipe Darryl's phone, and trust me, that's not a good idea."

"Boone," she whispered, pleading.

He rotated his head and looked at her again. "Shouldn't you be moaning by now?"

"No!" she whispered. "I'm quite sure I should not."

"A nice loud yee-haw, then," he suggested with a grin.

"I do not yee-haw," she said primly.

"Oh, that's too bad." Boone's grin faded. His eyelids seemed to grow heavy.

Boone rocked so hard the headboard banged against the wall. And again. He moved faster, harder, and a mortified Jayne, who did not think she could watch this indecent display any longer, tried to turn away from him.

And rolled off the bed. She squealed and landed on the floor with a thud.

The gyrations of the bed came to a sudden stop, and a moment later a grinning Boone glanced over the side. "Well, that was different. But okay. The guys will just think we had a quickie."

"That was not..." Jayne began, and then she pursed her lips. She considered sleeping on the floor herself tonight, but there was a draft. It was cold down here! Boone offered a helping hand, which she ignored. His grin faded and he stared at her, his expression hard and dark.

The fall must have addled her brain. Jayne suddenly realized that she was lying on the floor wearing nothing but her slip and panties, and in the fall the slip had ridden up high on her thighs. "Do you mind?" she said coolly, fluttering her fingers in Boone's direction.

"Pardon me, ma'am," he said, deepening his Southern accent and shifting away.

Jayne gathered what was left of her dignity and crawled back beneath the covers, while Boone remained on top. As soon as she was situated, he sat up and pulled off his black T-shirt.

"It's awfully chilly to be sleeping without...something on."

He tossed the shirt aside and lay back down. "I'll be fine. Nice of you to be concerned for me, though." There was just a touch of sarcasm in that last sentence.

At least he kept his jeans on. When he reached over and turned off the bedside lamp and they were left in darkness, Jayne breathed a sigh of relief. Maybe if she didn't have to look at him, she wouldn't be so...so distracted.

"I'm not being silly in wanting to call my parents," she whispered.

"I know. They're bound to be worried."

"That's true, but I'm also anxious about what my father might do. If this area is overrun with federal agents, army, navy, marines..."

"Navy in Arizona?" Boone asked, humor in his deep voice.

"Probably," she said softly.

"We'll be fine," he assured her.

How could she tell Boone that if he got killed or hurt because she'd been in the wrong place at the wrong time, she'd never forgive herself? There was more than one danger to worry about. If Darryl found out who she was and that Jim had survived, they were both in trouble. If they actually did get out of here and Boone was mistaken for a kidnapper, he might be dead before she had a chance to explain things.

Apparently Boone didn't want to talk anymore. Just as well. The man confused her. He looked like a criminal, he cursed too much, he was crude and wicked. But he was also one of the good guys. An angel. A modern-day knight.

More than that, he was sexy as all get-out. The smile, the eyes, the body. A quickie? She knew what a quickie was, thank you very much. Her one sexual experience had lasted less than two minutes, and it had been painful and unpleasant. She hadn't minded at the time, because she'd thought the man who had asked her to marry him actually loved her, and that things would get better with time.

But she and Dustin Talbot hadn't had time. She'd found out too soon that the only reason he'd asked her to marry him was that he had political ambitions, and being married to Gus Barrington's daughter would be a real boost for his career.

Since her recovery from that disastrous encounter, she'd been cautiously guarding her heart and waiting. Waiting for the perfect man to come along. Waiting for her knight in shining armor to appear.

She might occasionally think of Boone as a kind of errant knight, but he was far from perfect.

Maybe she'd waited too long. She was twenty-seven years old, and no man had ever made her moan or shake or shout yee-haw.

As Jayne drifted toward sleep, she chastised herself. She'd be lucky to survive the coming days, and here she was worried about her sex life! Or lack thereof.

But once, just once, she'd like to shout yee-haw.

Boone awoke slowly, reluctant to return to the world of the waking. He'd feel better if he didn't have to sleep at all, at least not on this job. He didn't trust Darryl. And Darryl didn't trust anyone.

There were four of them living in this shack, five if you counted Jayne, and yet there was only one working cell phone. Darryl's. One car. Darryl's. This shack was well off the beaten path, and whenever anyone needed to go to the nearest poor excuse for a town, usually for food or beer, he was not allowed to go alone. They traveled in pairs, always.

Setting up his cover here had taken time, but thanks to Dean and Luther, he'd had the paper trail and the contacts to make it work. An introduction from a snitch who hadn't yet been retired or caught had brought Boone, as Richard Becker, into the circle that Darryl ran and worked. And Darryl was his only key to finding Gurza.

As he came fully awake, Boone realized he was warm. Very nicely, unusually warm. Jayne was using his chest as a pillow. Her head rested over his heart, and one arm was draped around him. She breathed deeply and evenly, and had thrown the covers off so the sheet was partially twisted around both of them. Most of the green comforter had fallen off the foot of the bed.

He should think of Jayne as nothing more than a nuisance. That was all she was. She had stumbled onto something ugly, and in doing so she'd complicated an already difficult job. That aside, Jayne Barrington was everything he didn't like in a woman. Petite. Classy. Spoiled. Prudish. Rich. *Dainty*.

It was this make-believe relationship, he supposed, that made him occasionally look at her and wish that some of what he pretended was real.

He touched Jayne's red-gold curls and gently shifted her head. Comfy as this was, it definitely wasn't a good idea. "Wake up, sugar," he whispered.

She murmured against his chest, wriggled a little and didn't wake up.

His physical reaction to finding a half-dressed, pretty woman clinging to him in the morning, especially when he hadn't had sex in months, was completely natural, he was certain. Perfectly understandable. Somehow he had to get this woman off him. Now.

"Jayne," he said a little more loudly, patting her on the back this time.

She stirred finally, lifting her head to look him in the eye, whispering, "Yee…," before coming fully awake.

Realizing where she was, Jayne rolled quickly away. "How dare you?" she asked in that prim voice she used when she was really annoyed.

"Pardon me, miss priss, but you will notice that I'm on my side of the bed and have been all night."

She had no argument for that.

"Don't worry about it," he said as he left the bed. "You probably just got cold." *Or lonely.* "No big deal."

"Sorry," she said softly.

Darryl was probably already up and about. Maybe the boys, too. He really should grab the headboard and shake the bed and tease Jayne until she squealed. But he couldn't. No way. Not now. He grabbed his pistol from the bedside table and stood. "I'm going to take a shower." A *cold* one. "Lock the door behind me. Don't let anyone in but me."

"Don't worry," she muttered.

Once he was in the hallway, he listened until he heard the lock turn. He knew Jayne wouldn't open that door to anyone but him, but still he rushed through his shower. One way to get his mind off inappropriate speculation was to get his mind back on business.

Gurza had the kid, he knew it. Felt it in his gut. Maybe he was so damned certain because he knew if he didn't find the boy with Gurza, he'd probably never recover him at all, and that wasn't an option. So Boone could not let himself get distracted.

When he exited the shower, resolve strengthened, and headed for the kitchen, he noticed that Darryl was awake and sitting on the couch in the living room, staring at the space where his television had been.

"You owe me a television, Becker," the big man growled as Boone made a beeline for the coffee that smelled so good.

"When this is over, I'll buy you a big-screen TV,"

Boone said loudly enough for his voice to carry from the kitchen.

"You'll have the money for it," Darryl said, "once you start doing business with Gurza."

Darryl and the elusive Gurza thought Richard Becker was looking to expand his territory from the Atlanta area to all of Georgia and into Alabama. Since Gurza operated primarily in the Southwest, he was definitely interested in a piece of that action.

Darryl had been working with Gurza long enough to have a nice little bundle of his own somewhere. But for this meeting and subsequent deal, a low profile was called for. They didn't want to call any attention to themselves. Another reason the deal gone wrong really chapped Darryl's butt.

"I'm thinking of sending the boys out this afternoon to get me a TV," Darryl grumbled as Boone stepped into the living room. "I don't like this. The radio doesn't pick up much of anything out here, just that one easy-listening station."

Boone's heart climbed into his throat. "Afraid something important might be happening in the world of fashion and entertainment and you're missing it?" he said sarcastically. "Wondering what the weather's going to be like tomorrow? Besides," he added, "you said we were to stick close for these last few days. Do you really want to send those two idiots out to buy a television?"

Darryl looked up and around to glare at Boone. "One of those idiots is my nephew."

"I know that," Boone said. "But he's still an idiot."

Darryl just shrugged. "Besides, they're not going to buy one. They're going to break into an empty house and steal one."

The very idea made Boone sweat. What if the house turned out not to be empty? What if, once again, things went wrong? "Oh, yeah, great way to keep a low profile. Steal someone's television. Get the cops and the locals all stirred up."

Darryl didn't like having his authority questioned. "I have a particular house in mind. It's a vacation home, and the couple that stays there a few months out of the year have gone home. No one will know. No one will get stirred up."

"You've given this a lot of thought," Boone said as he sipped at his coffee.

"I don't like being out of touch."

Every curse word Boone knew flitted through his mind. Jayne would have been horrified.

"When are the boys going out?"

"This afternoon." Darryl grinned. "Wanna ride along?"

And leave Jayne here with Darryl? No way. "No thanks."

She didn't have much choice but to wear one of Boone's T-shirts, at least for a little while. Her suit was to be dry-cleaned only, so she couldn't do much about that, but her slip, blouse, bra and panties needed to be washed. Badly. The hose she'd simply thrown away.

Jayne cringed as she used liquid hand soap to wash her delicate things. The soap was surely much too harsh, but it would have to do. While she was in the middle of lathering and rinsing her things, Boone hammered on the door.

"Just a minute."

"No," he said. "Let me in. Now."

"I'm almost—"

"Now!"

She reached across and unlocked the bathroom door, and as Boone walked in and slammed the door behind him, locking it once again, she finished rinsing and wringing out her delicates.

"What are you doing?" Boone asked with a shake of his head.

"What does it look like I'm doing?" She kept her eyes on the last of her work as she wrung out her panties and hung them up to dry. She should be embarrassed, and she was, a little. But considering the situation, she didn't think she needed to overreact just because Boone was staring at her panties.

He shook his head again and glared at her. "I told you to stay in the room."

"No, you didn't. You told me not to let anyone but you in. I peeked into the hallway and no one was there, so I ran down to the bathroom and locked myself in here. I just needed to rinse out a few things."

His eyes raked over her body. Jayne didn't flinch. She was perfectly decent in one of Boone's many black T-shirts. It was baggy and hung almost to her knees. It was actually longer than her coral skirt.

He moved closer, leaned over her and whispered in her ear. "We have to get out of here today."

Her heart lurched. She wanted out of this place more than she'd ever wanted anything, but a necessary escape meant something had gone wrong. "Why?"

"Darryl's sending the boys out to steal a TV this afternoon. As soon as they see the news and find out who you are, we're done."

"Darn," she mumbled.

"My thought exactly," Boone said gruffly.

Jayne's heart lurched when someone tried the doorknob. The jiggling of the knob was followed by a sharp knock.

Boone grumbled, "Hold your horses."

Just as Jayne automatically said, "Just a minute."

Doug called out. "I gotta take a leak."

"Go outside!" Boone shouted. "We're not…finished."

"Jeez," Doug complained as he moved down the hallway. "It's like living with a couple of rabbits."

When Doug was gone and the hallway was silent again, Jayne looked into Boone's eyes. He was angry and he was very frustrated. Taking care of her had ruined this case, on which he'd spent months. Judging by the sober expression on his face, he probably wished, at least a little, that he'd let Darryl shoot her.

"I'm sorry," she whispered.

"Me, too."

"Maybe you could let me get away and…stay here to finish what you started?"

Boone shook his head slowly. "If I let you get away, Darryl will kill me on the spot."

"Oh," she breathed, her heart kicking again.

There was another footstep in the hallway, another knock on the door.

"One minute!" Boone said testily.

"Sorry," Marty called.

"What do we do?" Jayne asked, leaning into Boone and whispering softly.

"You're not in there alone, are you, Becker?" Marty asked, more than a hint of teasing in his voice.

Boone stared down at Jayne, his long hair brushing his cheek, his corded neck telling her he was wound too tightly. "Get your stuff," he said, nodding toward the items she had drying on the shower-curtain rod.

"They're not dry."

He clenched his jaw. "If you want to keep anything that's hanging up there, bring it with you now."

No matter how dire the circumstances, she wasn't going to run without her underwear. Jayne quickly snapped all the wet items down, wondering as she did so what Boone would do next. Would he conjure up some kind of noise to make Marty think they were fooling around in the bathroom? Maybe pick her up as they left the tiny room and impatiently carry her down the hallway?

In the end, he didn't do anything but open the door and take her arm as he led her back to the bedroom. And still, Marty snickered.

Chapter 5

Boone ejected the magazine from the butt of his Colt and examined it quickly. Fully loaded, as he'd known it would be. He had hopes that maybe, just maybe, they could get out of here without the escape turning messy. He had to be ready just in case they weren't so lucky. He stuck the pistol in the waistband of his jeans and shrugged on his leather jacket.

They'd talked it over. Twice. Jayne knew exactly what she was supposed to do. He glanced at her. She stood by the window, looking out on another sunny Arizona afternoon. She hadn't complained, but she was scared.

He couldn't blame her.

She looked different than she had when he'd first seen her. For one thing, she wore one of his black T-shirts with her slim peach skirt, pearls and pumps. Her hair was curlier than it had been when he'd caught her running from the scene of Jim's shooting. She'd washed her hair and let it dry naturally, bemoaning the lack of a hair dryer, and the curls went this way and that. She didn't like it. He did.

She didn't bother with makeup now, since all she had in her purse was lipstick and mascara. Jayne didn't need makeup. Her skin was like silk, and her lips didn't need artificial color.

Any man might be distracted, especially if he had her still-damp panties and bra stuffed in the pocket of his jacket, as Boone did.

"Ready, sugar?"

Jayne nodded.

Doug and Marty were running their errand, which meant they'd only have Darryl to deal with. Darryl usually took an afternoon nap. Boone crossed his fingers that this was one of those afternoons.

He took Jayne's arm and they stepped into the living room. Sure enough, Darryl was sleeping on the couch, his head on the armrest, his feet hanging over the end.

Boone and Jayne turned, arm in arm still, toward the kitchen. They hadn't taken two steps before the couch creaked. Boone closed his eyes and cursed silently.

"Where the hell do you two think you're going?"

Jayne had left her purse, blouse and slip behind, but wore her suit jacket over the T-shirt. They didn't want to look as if they were leaving for good.

Boone turned to face Darryl as the fat man came to his feet. "We're going for a walk." Easily, and as if he was hiding the gesture from Jayne, he laid his hand over the butt of his pistol.

"Why don't you wait until the boys get back?" Darryl scratched his massive belly. "They might want to *walk* with you."

Boone shook his head. "No."

Jayne, playing her part perfectly, reached out and grabbed his arm. "Is something wrong, BooBoo? You don't seem very happy today. We don't have to go for a walk. I can make you something to eat or rub your back or...or wash your clothes or—"

"Enough," Boone snapped, rolling his eyes.

Darryl grinned, buying their ploy that Jayne was getting just a little bit too clingy for her captor.

If everything went well, they'd walk toward the vast stretch of rugged unpopulated land that separated the shack from rolling hills and red rock formations in the distance. Darryl would be watching from the window, of that Boone was certain. When they were out of sight, Boone would fire one shot into the air. Darryl would be satisfied, thinking Jayne was dead.

But Boone wouldn't be returning to the shack. He and Jayne were going to keep moving, and by the time Darryl thought to look for him and the boys got back with the car and the television, Boone and Jayne would be long gone. He hoped.

He took Jayne's arm and escorted her through the kitchen and out the door. A gust of wind met them. It wouldn't be an easy walk, but they'd be fine. Anything was better than facing Darryl and his boys once they knew the truth.

They circled the shack, and Jayne got a good look at the landscape they'd be crossing on foot. It wasn't going to be easy, he knew, but it was the best chance they had.

He'd studied this area, and he knew they'd be all right. Might have a few rough hours, but in the end Jayne would be safe...and he'd be back to square one. Dammit, he had no idea how to start over, how to get to Gurza now that his hard-won association with Darryl was finished.

His first hint that things were not going as planned was the sound of footsteps behind them. "He's following us," Boone muttered.

"I know," Jayne whispered. "Now what?"

Without thinking, Boone cursed.

Jayne cleared her throat in a not-so-subtle reminder that she didn't like that word.

"Fudge," he growled. "I have no idea now what," he said softly. "I should have known that Darryl would have to see this with his own eyes." His step didn't falter. "If I say run, you go. Don't question me, don't hesitate. Just run. You head for those hills over there." He looked toward their destination but did not nod his head. "You don't stop, you don't slow down."

"But what if you—"

"And don't look back," he interrupted. "Whatever you do, don't look back."

Her steps faltered a little on the uneven terrain, but she said nothing.

"Far enough," he said, coming to a halt.

Jayne looked up at him, fear and strength and indecision in her eyes. Green eyes with a touch of blue. Blue flecks he hadn't seen so well in the dimly lit room he'd shared with her for two nights and one and a half days.

She reached up and bracketed his face with her hands. Her fingers trembled, and the caress of those hands was so soft and tender something deep in his gut went thud. Without saying a word, she rose on her toes and laid her mouth over his. She kissed him. Not a passionate, tongues-dueling kiss, but something sweet and intoxicating and breathtaking.

Out of the corner of his eye, Boone saw Darryl approaching. Gritty dirt kicked up with each step, and Darryl laid his massive hand on his own weapon, a revolver tucked into his waistband.

When Jayne ended the kiss and dropped down to stand flat-footed once again, Boone laid his hand over the butt of his weapon. "Run."

She did. Without hesitation she turned and ran toward the hills. Boone drew his Colt and took aim.

"Fire," Darryl said.

"Now where's the sport in that?" Boone grinned and closed one eye as he aimed at Jayne. "I'm going to give her a few more feet."

He stood there and watched Jayne run. She didn't look back; good girl. She ran as fast as she could, but he had a sinking feeling it wasn't fast enough.

Darryl cursed and drew his own weapon. Boone, anticipating the move, spun and kicked the weapon out of Darryl's hand.

The fat man howled and grabbed his wrist. "You're letting her get away!"

When Boone still made no move to shoot Jayne, Darryl bent down to retrieve his weapon. Boone spun again and kicked Darryl—in the jaw this time. Darryl was caught by surprise, and at the moment it didn't matter how big he was. Boone's heavy boot, with the proper force behind it, was too much for him. He jerked up and twirled around, before falling to the ground, flat on his ugly face. Unconscious.

Boone scooped up Darryl's gun and ran, following Jayne's path. It didn't take him long to catch up with her. When he did he saw tears streaming down her cheeks. She turned her head to look at him and sniffled as her pace slowed.

"Is he dead?"

Boone shook his head. "No. Killing someone, even Darryl, would only land me in a world of trouble."

"Are you…" She continued to run, even though she hadn't stopped crying. "Are you hurt?"

Boone grinned and held his arms out wide, to show Jayne that he was unhurt. He held one weapon in each hand, his and Darryl's.

Jayne stopped crying and she also stopped running. Just as well. They had a long way to go and there was no way they could run the whole time. "You're an imbecile," she said, her face going pale. "You might have gotten yourself killed back there!"

"I'm fine," he said. "You're fine. We're both fine."

She gave an indignant snort, and then her expression softened. "I thought you were going to get yourself shot."

Jayne had been worried. She hadn't cried once since this whole debacle got under way, but she'd cried for him.

He shook off any hint of an idea that she might care about him. Women like Jayne, they cared about everyone and everything, right? Feed the world. Free the whales. Cure the disease of the moment. Worrying about a P.I. with a death wish was just another cause to add to her list of things to do.

And it didn't matter at the moment that she wasn't his type, that if not for chance they never would have met, that they lived in worlds so different they probably wouldn't be able to function together outside disaster mode. None of that mattered. He still wanted to add Jayne to *his* list of things to do.

Boone insisted that they move quickly. Darryl was out cold at the moment, but there was no telling when

he might come to or what he would do when he did.
Boone seemed to think they had a small window in
which to put some distance between them and the
shack. For one thing, Darryl was going to have to get
another weapon and wait for the boys to return. He
wouldn't take off after them on his own.

He didn't hang on to Darryl's gun. When they were
far from the shack, he stopped and emptied the gun of
bullets and pocketed them. He dismantled the weapon
quickly and efficiently, then threw the pieces in three
different directions. That done, they resumed their jog.

Jayne's feet were already killing her. Her coral
pumps were not made for running. Her heart beat too
hard, as much from the fear of wondering what
might've happened to Boone back there as from their
pace. It had been his instruction not to look back that
got to her.

Boone might have died just to get her out of that
place and away from Darryl, and he didn't seem to give
that sacrifice any significant thought at all. She'd known
him two days, and he was willing to put his life on the
line for her.

Not just for her, she imagined, but for any damsel in
distress. Boone Sinclair definitely had the knight-in-
shining-armor complex.

He jogged beside and just ahead of her, that long hair
dancing, the sound of his footsteps solid on the uneven
ground. She'd always imagined sand when she thought
of Arizona desert, but this rough landscape was brown
and rugged, dotted here and there with interesting, bar-
ren-looking red rock formations. No sand, no blooming
cacti. Still, if she wasn't so tired she might find it beautiful.

"I need to take a breather," she said, slowing to a walk.

Boone turned around. "No time for a breather, not if we want to make Rockvale by nightfall."

"Just a minute," she said. "Please."

He stopped and so did she, and with a critical eye he looked her up and down. His eyes stopped on her feet. "I wish we could have rounded you up a good pair of boots. Tennis shoes, at the very least. Why on earth did you wear such impractical shoes?"

She loved her pumps! "Sorry," she said softly, "but when I left the hotel in Flagstaff, I really didn't plan for this contingency."

He grinned and turned his back to her, then dropped down to his haunches. "Jump on."

"I will not!"

He glanced over his shoulder, smile gone. "We can't just stand here and wait for Darryl. You don't weigh much. I can carry you for a while."

Tentatively and without dignity, she climbed onto Boone's back, her arms snaking around his neck. He snagged her legs as he rose to his feet, so that he caught her under the knees.

"I haven't ridden like this since I was eight and my dad took me hiking."

Boone started jogging. "Don't tell me," he said. "You wore tiny little high-heeled shoes."

"No." She smiled. "I just got tired."

They quit talking. Since Boone was jogging and carrying her, he probably didn't have the air in his lungs to carry on a conversation. She didn't have anything to say, not really. Here she dangled, literally wrapped around a man who was, in spite of everything that had happened, a stranger. Why did she trust him? Why did she believe everything he had told her? She had no real reason to trust Boone Sinclair, but she did.

Jayne's eyes scanned the rough terrain. There were snakes here, she knew it. Rattlers, for sure, and probably other little sneaky poisonous snakes that didn't bother to warn unsuspecting joggers with a rattling of their tails. There were surely other critters close by, too, but she didn't worry about them. But the snakes...

The hills Boone ran toward seemed to get no closer. The small town of Rockvale was on the other side of those hills, according to him. Once there they would make a few phone calls and this would be over.

Well, it would be over for her. Boone's job, whatever had brought him here, was unfinished. Thanks to her. Would he go back to complete what he'd started? Surely not. It would be foolishly dangerous to do such a thing.

He turned and headed for the shade of a rock outcropping to his right, and once there he dipped down so Jayne could slip off him and stand.

A nice breeze kept the afternoon from being too warm, but come nightfall it would be cold. She knew that. They couldn't stop here for long, but Boone certainly needed to rest.

He reached into an inside pocket of his leather jacket and pulled out a small bottle of water. The man thought of everything. He uncapped it and handed it to her. Jayne took a quick sip and returned the bottle to him; he surely needed water more than she did.

He took not much more than a sip before reaching into another inside pocket and drawing out a pack of cheese crackers. He opened the pack and gave her one.

"I'm not hungry," she said.

"Eat it. At this rate, we'll be later than I figured

getting to town. I don't want you getting weak from hunger.''

She ate the cracker, took another sip of water and looked toward the hills. ''I should walk on my own for a while,'' she said. ''You can't carry me all the way.''

He grinned as if none of this mattered. ''You don't weigh much.''

''Enough,'' she said. ''It can't be…''

Boone's easy smile faded and he held up a hand to silence her. He looked back the way they'd come and squinted. Then he muttered a very foul word.

''Fudge,'' she reminded him. Again.

He laid long-suffering eyes on her. ''I hear motorcycle engines, and I see dust clouds headed this way.''

Jayne felt a little dizzy. No matter what kind of shoes she was wearing, she couldn't outrun motorcycles. Neither could Boone.

Boone searched the area carefully, his gaze scanning everything and finally going up. ''There,'' he said, pointing high above Jayne's head.

Jayne tilted her head back. There was a narrow crevice in the wall of rock. It was a good twenty feet up. ''We might be able to hide in that…cave, or whatever it is,'' she conceded. ''But how on earth are we supposed to get up there?''

''We climb.'' He wasn't about to argue or cajole. There was no time. He grabbed Jayne and gave her a boost. ''There are plenty of footholds in the wall. You just have to find them.''

Jayne's survival instinct helped her to very quickly find places to hang on with her hands and with her feet. It was not a secure feeling. At Boone's insistent urging, she found a foothold a little higher and inched her way up.

She proceeded that way, Boone directly behind her, her eyes on the crevice above, for what seemed like hours but had to be minutes. Now she heard the motorcycle engines, too.

"What if I fall?" she asked breathlessly.

"I'll catch you."

She wanted to look down at Boone but didn't dare. "You can't catch me! We'll both fall!"

"Then don't let go," he said tightly.

He was just beneath her, urging her up, prodding her to move more quickly. Once or twice he physically prodded her with a large hand to her backside.

"What if the motorcycles you hear are law-enforcement officers looking for me?" she asked breathlessly.

"If we see them and they're official, we'll call out and you'll be properly rescued. If we don't determine that they've been sent by Daddy, we sit still and assume they're working with Darryl."

"The boys," she muttered. "Drat!" she drew one hand briefly away from the rock wall.

"What's wrong?" Boone asked.

"I broke a nail," Jayne said, resuming her slow climb.

Behind her, Boone laughed softly.

"It's not funny!"

"Of course it isn't."

Her foot slipped once, and somehow Boone caught and steadied her ankle with his hand.

"I'm not an outdoorsy person," she said, frustrated. Her arms and legs ached, and she couldn't breathe deeply.

"No kidding," Boone said.

"I don't think I can make it."

"We're almost there. Keep moving, sugar." This encouragement was aided by another shove of his hand to her backside.

Jayne moved up a few more inches. "Would you *please* keep your *hands* off my *ass!*"

"Yes, ma'am." More than a touch of humor colored his low voice. "You move it, and I'll keep my hands off it."

She climbed faster, as fast as she could, and finally, hallelujah, she reached the crevice. She glanced inside before scurrying in, well aware that her skirt was too short and too narrow for climbing into a cave in a ladylike manner. She was not dressed for crawling over rock. A couple of times, she'd thought about asking Boone for her underwear. Surely they were dry by now! But she hadn't asked. The time and the mood had never been quite right for such an embarrassing request. As she made her way into the small cave, her right shoe slipped off and fell.

Jayne scooted all the way to the back of the small cave, and Boone scrambled in after her. Almost immediately she saw that he had her lost shoe in one hand. She breathed a sigh of relief. At least they wouldn't have to worry about the searchers—if they were indeed Darryl's men—finding evidence that she had been here. She leaned back against the cool stone wall and brought her knees up not quite to her chest. She reached out her hand, silently asking for her coral pump, but Boone grabbed her by the ankle and slipped the shoe on.

First her rear end, now her foot. "Really, Boone..." she began.

He placed a finger to his lips and then leaned close. Too close. And whispered. "Sounds carry out here, and whoever's on those motorcycles is almost here."

She whispered into Boone's ear, moving a long length of dark brown hair out of her way. "I doubt very much they can hear me over the motorcycle engines."

As if in answer to her very logical argument, the engines that roared out there in the wilderness died.

Chapter 6

Boone didn't move. He rested one hand on Jayne's knee and listened carefully.

Whoever was out there had parked their motorcycles and were searching the area on foot. There were two of them, by the sound of things, and they had stopped to search around the red rocks, to reach uneven and craggy places where the motorcycles could not go. If they decided to climb up and search this cave, he and Jayne were in big trouble.

Boone laid one hand over the pistol at his gut. If anyone stuck their head in this cave, he just might have to blow it off.

A voice drifted up. "Nothin'. They ain't here."

Jayne stiffened. Apparently she'd recognized Doug's voice, too.

"Yeah," Marty said. "I think while Darryl was passed out, Becker grabbed the woman and they headed

in another direction. We would have found them by
now if they were out here.''

"Maybe," Doug said. "Lots of places to hide, I
reckon.''

Boone listened and waited, but the boys didn't move
on. "We can't head back yet," Marty said. "Darryl will
have our hides if we show up too soon.''

"I know. Maybe if we wait out here a while, some
of those boys Darryl has checking out Meeker will find
something.''

Boone breathed a sigh of relief. Darryl had sent men
to search the town that was situated a few miles closer
to the shack than Rockvale, the one-stoplight crossroads
he and Jayne were headed to. He'd known Darryl would
search Meeker, which is the reason he and Jayne were
not going there. He'd still have to be careful, though.
Darryl could easily expand the search to include Rockvale.

Darryl must really be furious if he was calling on
other men and bringing in motorcycles for the boys to
use in the search. Darryl liked to keep his circle of
"friends" small.

"You know," Marty said, sounding puzzled. "I
never took Becker as the sort to go soft over a woman.
I mean, he blew a really big deal for a *girl*.''

"She musta been good," Doug mused.

Boone glanced at Jayne and saw that she had her lips
pursed and her knees locked together.

"No woman's that good.''

The boys settled in for a conversation about their own
limited sexual experiences, comparing notes. Embellish-
ing their most memorable encounters. Boone looked at
Jayne once and found her blushing and staring straight
ahead, glaring at the fascinating sight of a stone wall.

Well, apparently they didn't know yet who Jayne was or that Jim was alive. The escape had taken them away from their newly stolen TV and the news, he imagined. Didn't really matter. They'd find out soon enough.

He sat there for a while—one hand on the butt of his pistol, the other on Jayne's knee—feeling strangely grounded. Doug and Marty's topic of conversation changed, thank God, to something safe and ordinary. Soap operas.

Eventually Jayne relaxed a little. He felt the change come over her, like a wave of serenity passing through her body. After a few minutes she rested her head against his arm.

"Sleep, if you want," he whispered. "We might be here awhile."

She didn't speak, but she did nod her head and close her eyes.

The woman was amazing. Prudish, annoying, short-tempered…and amazing. She had weathered this crisis more bravely than many men he knew would have, never falling apart, never wailing—unless he pinched her. And she slept easily and deeply. Her life was on the line, and still she slept. She slept because she naively trusted him to take care of her, to get her out of this mess alive and unhurt.

He didn't deserve that trust. Jayne would do well to learn that it wasn't safe to put her life in anyone's hands. Least of all his.

She sighed, and in her sleep she nuzzled her cheek against his arm.

Amazing.

Several things happened at once. Jayne heard the distant sound of motorcycle engines, a hand nudged her, and she opened her eyes to discover that she no longer slept with her cheek on Boone's arm, but was curled up with her cheek resting on his thigh.

She sat up quickly, trying to ignore the awkward position she'd awakened in. "It's almost dark," she said, looking out the cave entrance.

"Yeah. If we don't climb down soon, we'll be stuck here all night."

Jayne's heart thumped. She didn't think she could bear to spend the night with Boone in these close quarters. So close, so tight, he seemed bigger than ever, more menacing. Not menacing in the sense she'd felt when she'd thought he was a criminal intent on killing her, but menacing just the same.

He took her hand and they left the cave, but they didn't go down the way they'd come up. A very narrow ledge sloped slightly down and then up again. Holding her hand, as if that might actually do any good if she fell, Boone very carefully made his way across the ledge. Jayne watched her every step. There was no room for error.

The sun had set, and they had very little light to make their way by. Soon they'd have nothing but moonlight. The ledge curved around the rock, and on the other side it ended abruptly.

Boone didn't seem disturbed by the fact. He very easily released her hand and then jumped to a ledge four or five feet below. Jayne's heart almost stopped as she watched him.

"Great," she said. "Now you're down there and I'm up here!"

Boone smiled at her and offered his arms. "Jump."

"I can't!"

"You can."

Moving with great care, she took off her shoes and tossed them down. Boone caught one and then the other, then set them down. Jayne tried to lower herself to sit on the ledge, but there was simply not enough ledge.

"Jump, sugar," Boone said confidently.

Jayne took a deep breath and did just that. She jumped. She wanted to close her eyes, but didn't. As promised, Boone caught her, his arms solid and strong, his strength never wavering. She looked up into his eyes and he smiled, and then he released her and retrieved her shoes.

The rest of the journey down was easier. There was another ledge, which was a bit wider than the one higher up, and then there was a series of rocks to which they hopped down and across.

When Jayne's feet landed on solid gritty dirt, she was tempted to get down on her knees and kiss the ground.

Boone took her hand once again and they resumed their trek. She liked the feel of her hand in his, the easy connection, the sharing of strength. She'd been escorted lots of places in her adult life, usually by up-and-coming politicians and eager lawyers, but there hadn't been much hand-holding going on. It was nice. Very nice.

"How long before we get to this little town?" she asked.

"A few hours."

Hours. Jayne took a deep breath and told herself, silently, that she could do this. The past couple of days had been tough, but the ordeal was almost over. As she walked she thought of all the things she'd do when she got back to her hotel. A hot bath, a decent meal, a good bottle of wine. All this would come after she'd called home of course.

There were so many things she'd taken for granted. Safety. Freedom. The promise of another day, always. She didn't think she could ever take those things for granted again.

"What are you going to do now?" she asked.

Boone continued to walk, always a step or two ahead of her. "Once we get to Rockvale we'll get something to eat, then—"

"No," she said. "About the case you were working on."

He was silent for a few steps. "I don't know. I haven't decided."

"Can I…help?"

The offer made him glance back. "No, I don't think so. But thanks for offering."

"Goodness, I don't even know what kind of case it is! But I would be willing to help if I could."

Boone didn't take the hint and tell her what he was working on. Jayne made a childish face at his back. Stubborn man!

"What are you going to do when you get back to civilization?" he asked.

"Take a bath," she muttered.

He laughed lightly. "And after that?"

With the setting of the sun, the temperature of the air had dropped. Her jacket blocked most of the chill, but not all. She shivered as she contemplated the question. "First thing, even before the bath, I need to call my folks and let them know I'm okay."

"Naturally. And I guess after that you'll pay a visit to your friend Jim, the guy Darryl shot."

She didn't care if she ever saw Jim again. "Can't I just send him flowers and be done with it? Oh, that sounds terrible, I shouldn't have said that, but…I do want him to be okay. I just don't want him to think we're going to be friends from now on because of this." She sighed. "That does sound terribly rude, doesn't it?"

"Not the best blind date you ever had, I'm guessing," Boone teased.

"Not even close. My friend Pamela lives in Flagstaff. I don't get to see her often, but we talk on the phone and e-mail a lot. We went to school together and were in the same sorority."

Boone shook his head. "Sorority. I should have figured."

She reached out and slapped him lightly on the arm. "There's nothing wrong with being in a sorority."

"Of course not." He sounded unconvinced.

"Anyway, Pamela fixes me up with Jim, since we're both single and she can't stand the thought of anyone not being as happily married as she is. It's her new quest in life to see me married and pregnant."

Boone glanced at her, raked his eyes up and down as his smile died. Jayne was quite sure that no one had ever looked at her this way before. Oh, she wanted to know what Boone was thinking, but he didn't have the kind of expressive face that gave his thoughts away. He was solid, stoic. Real. More real than any man she'd ever known.

"You're cold," he said, coming to a halt and shrugging off his leather jacket.

"No," she protested. "You can't…you can't walk all the way to town in a short-sleeved shirt! You'll catch your death of cold out here."

"I'm cold-blooded, like those snakes you hate so much." He held out the jacket and would not be dissuaded. Finally Jayne offered her arms and he helped her slip the jacket on.

Cold-blooded? Not likely. The jacket was warm. Boone was warm. He was no snake.

He turned around and dropped to his haunches. "Hop on."

"Boone—"

"We'll get there quicker this way, and jogging will keep me warm."

"All right." Jayne climbed onto his back and held on tight. No, Boone Sinclair was definitely not cold-blooded.

The lights of Rockvale, though few, were a welcome sight. Since it wasn't the closest town to the shack where he'd been staying, he hadn't been here and shouldn't be recognized. Just in case someone out there was looking for a man and a woman together, he made Jayne wait out of sight while he secured a room in the town's only motel, a seedy place if ever he'd seen one.

He paid cash and gave the man at the desk a false name. Smith.

As soon as they walked into the motel room, Jayne kicked off her shoes and took off his jacket. "I wonder if they have room service here."

He smiled at her back. "I don't think so."

Jayne headed directly for the phone, reaching out for the receiver.

Boone moved quickly and was there before she could lift it. "Wait." He laid his hand over hers.

Jayne looked up at him. "You know I have to call my family."

"We don't know what kind of equipment or personnel Darryl is using to find us."

"One phone call—"

"If he traces us here before I have reinforcements in place, we're done. We're dead, sugar."

She went pale. "Surely he wouldn't have the facilities to trace a phone call."

"Darryl, no. The man I came here looking for, yes. If Darryl has enlisted his help, it's possible there's a tap on your dad's phone. There might be a tap on the telephones of everyone you know and might call."

"Surely not so soon…"

"We can't take that chance."

Jayne sat on the side of the single bed in the room. She looked deflated.

"I'm going to get us something to eat," he said. "And while I'm out, I'll use a pay phone to call a friend of mine who's with the DEA." He'd been thinking as they finished their journey, trying to get his mind off the woman he carried on his back. He had a plan, and with any luck Del and his partner would be in Flagstaff by morning. "I'll get a message to your family that you're all right and will call them tomorrow."

With a deep breath, Jayne relaxed. "That will do, I suppose."

"So," Boone said as he looked around the crummy room where they'd spend the night. It wasn't nice even by his standards, but everything they'd need was here. A television, a clock radio, a bathroom and a bed. Again, *one* bed. "I don't know what I'll find for supper, but I'll come back with something to eat. And beer." Man, he needed a beer.

Jayne wrinkled her nose. "I don't like beer. But oh, I'd love a nice Merlot. And chocolate-chip cookies, the soft kind."

"Cookies and wine?"

She gave him a small enchanting smile. "I won't have them at the same time."

"Right." He grabbed his jacket from the foot of the bed and pulled it on. "Lock the door behind me."

She followed him to the door. "I know the drill by now," she said. "I won't let anyone in but you."

As soon as the door was bolted behind Boone, Jayne ran to the bathroom and started the water running. He probably wouldn't be gone long, so she wouldn't allow herself the long soak she wanted, but as she was unbearably filthy, a quick shower was definitely called for.

As she peeled off her suit jacket, she glanced at the phone. She did think Boone was being overly cautious in suggesting that her father's phones might be monitored. Surely it wasn't that easy to gain access to a U.S. senator's phone lines! But she had promised Boone that she would wait, and she would. If his friends could get word to her family that she was safe, that would have to do for now.

She stepped out of her skirt, noting that it would have to be disposed of. Too bad. She'd liked that suit, and she'd only worn it twice! Boone's black T-shirt came over her head next and was tossed aside. The water was surely hot by now.

The shower was quick, hot and heavenly. She lathered her hair, using the motel's shampoo, and worked up a lather with the motel soap. She had never in her life felt so grimy! If she had her way she'd never hike, jog or climb ever again.

She stepped out of the shower into a steamy room, and dried her hair with the motel hair dryer. When she was completely dry, feeling truly clean for the first time in days, she walked back into the bedroom and grabbed

Boone's T-shirt. She had nothing else to wear, so it would have to do.

She picked up and folded the coral suit—knowing she had no choice but to wear it again tomorrow—and turned on the television. After surfing through the five channels available and finding nothing interesting, she turned the television off again. When it was time for the news, she'd try again. She might not like what she saw, but she felt she needed to watch, anyway.

Jayne bounded off the bed. Where was Boone? She was starving. Ravenous. And she couldn't wait to down a nice big glass of Merlot. She busied herself cleaning off the single table in the room, moving aside the tourist guides and thin packets of information about the area. That done, she fetched two glasses from the bathroom and placed them on opposite sides of the table.

Steak, she thought as she sat in one of the chairs at that wobbly table. She would really, really love a steak.

When a knock finally sounded on the door, she almost neglected to look through the peephole. She knew that impatient knock already. But she did look, and it was, of course, Boone standing on the other side of the door.

With a smile on her face, Jayne threw open the door. "I hope you have steak and Merlot in that bag."

Boone just stood there, staring at her, his head cocked to one side as his eyes raked over her. He didn't come in. "You're naked," he muttered.

"I am not!" Maybe his T-shirt wasn't exactly proper attire, but she was definitely not naked.

Boone shook his head and came inside, handing her a heavy bag and bolting the door behind him. "No steak," he said, ignoring his "naked" comment. "The only place open was a convenience store, so dinner is cheese in a can, crackers and Vienna sausages.''

"Sounds wonderful," she said, meaning it. Hunger did that to a woman.

"And no Merlot." He placed the bag he still carried on the table and drew out a bottle of wine. "Maybe this will do."

"Strawberry," she said, trying not to sound surprised as she read the label on the cheap wine.

"And clean clothes," he said, reaching deep into the bag and drawing out two T-shirts.

"Oh, thank God!" she said gratefully taking the shirt he offered her. It was pale blue, a lovely color. "I'll be right back." She ran into the bathroom, closed the door, whipped off Boone's black T-shirt and pulled on the new, clean, blue T-shirt. Like the other one, this shirt hung almost to her knees. There was a saying emblazoned across the front: "If a man speaks in the forest and there's no woman there to hear him, is he still wrong?"

When she left the bathroom, she found Boone laying their dinner out on the table. Beer for him, strawberry wine for her. Paper plates for the crackers and Vienna sausages and aerosol cheese.

She nodded to the dark-green T-shirt he'd flung across the foot of the bed. "What does yours say?"

He stepped aside and lifted the shirt for her to read: "Change is good. You go first."

"Are you trying to make some kind of statement with your clothing choices?" she teased.

He shook his head. "It's not like they had a lot to choose from at the convenience store, and I didn't exactly have time to browse."

"Didn't they have anything black? That green is dark, but it is technically a color."

He mumbled something and she had to prod him before he'd answer loudly enough for her to hear.

"They had one black T-shirt," he admitted, "and it said something about PMS."

Normally she would be embarrassed, but instead of blushing and ignoring the comment, she laughed. It was rather funny, and besides, nothing about tonight was normal.

Boone held her chair out for her, and she sat down. He'd already poured her a glass of wine, and she took a sip as he claimed his own chair. Not bad.

"I talked to my friend in the DEA. He and his partner are on their way. I also made arrangements for someone to call your father."

"They're going to help you finish your case?"

Boone nodded.

"Good," Jayne said. "It's better that you have some help."

"Why?" He put food on his plate, opened his beer and took a long swallow.

Jayne didn't look at him, but put a few things on her own plate, as well. "It'll be safer that way, surely. You'll have someone to, you know, watch your back."

"I like working alone."

He liked danger, he meant. Playing cowboy. Taking on people like Darryl all by himself. "Well, that's… silly."

"Silly?" He obviously didn't care for the observation.

"Why take unnecessary chances?"

"Why not?"

"There might be people out there who care whether

or not you get your fool head blown off,'' she snapped.
She didn't want him thinking she was talking about herself, so she continued in a calmer voice, ''Don't you
have any family?''

''Oh, yeah,'' he replied. ''Two brothers, a sister, a
brother-in-law and a nephew on the way. My sister's
due next month.'' He sounded none too happy about
the prospect of being an uncle.

Jayne smiled. ''Oh, a *baby*.''

Boone shook his head. ''What is it with chicks and
babies?''

''Don't you like babies?''

He shook his head. ''What's to like? They can't do
anything for themselves, they're messy, they smell, and
they require constant care.''

''You'll feel different when you have kids of your
own.''

The expression on his face that came and went very
quickly was grim. ''None for me, thanks.''

They both ate in silence after that. Boone finished his
beer but didn't open another one. Jayne drank her entire
glass of strawberry wine, but didn't pour more. She was
tired already. She didn't want to be light-headed, as
well.

Finally Boone excused himself to take a shower of
his own, grabbing his new shirt off the bed and heading
for the bathroom, then closing the door forcefully behind him.

Chapter 7

Boone vigorously dried his hair. Bad ideas continued to plague him.

Jayne was probably a virgin. Of course she was. There had been that comment about *some* women making love silently, and in the beginning she really hadn't had much of a clue about what kind of noises to make while he shook the bed. Her best scream had come because she'd turned her mind to snakes.

She even kissed like a virgin, soft and sweet and… and like she was waiting for something to happen. Crap. He wanted absolutely nothing to do with a virgin. Ever.

"Boone!" Jayne pounded on the door as she called his name.

Something was wrong. Boone snagged a towel and quickly wrapped it around his waist, grabbed his gun from the back of the toilet and threw open the door, pistol in hand. "What's wrong?"

Jayne had already jumped into the bed, and she was straightening the covers over her legs. "Jim is on the news. Can you believe this guy?"

Boone lowered his weapon and turned to the TV, his heart still pounding. Sure enough, Jim was there, playing to the camera.

"Like I said, I tried to save Jayne from those monsters, but they jumped me. All six of them." He gestured wildly with his hands. "One of them shot me and I went down. After that, everything's a blank for a while."

An eager reporter asked another question. "And yet you managed to call for help."

Boone sighed. This was where it would get sticky. Once Darryl heard what happened…

"I came to long enough to have the presence of mind to dial 911," Jim said solemnly.

"What?"

"Shh." Jayne raised a silencing hand.

"*I* called 911," Boone whispered.

"I know."

"I'm sure those…those criminals," Jim went on, "thought I was dead when they left me there. When I regained consciousness, I was alone on the road. It took all the strength I could muster to take my cell phone out of my jacket pocket and dial, but I knew it was the only chance I had."

Boone grinned. "Thank you, Jimmy boy."

"Why are you thanking him?" Jayne asked sharply. "He just lied about…*everything*."

"I know, bless his devious, attention-hungry little heart." Boone placed his gun on the dresser near the television. He turned to face Jayne. Yeah, she looked too damn good, and she was most likely virginal, untouched territory. "If Darryl buys it, I'm off the hook. Maybe. I can tell him I had a moment of sexually induced weakness and helped you escape so he wouldn't shoot you, but he doesn't have to know I helped Jim. I can tell him I didn't feel a pulse." He shrugged. "Thinking Jim was dead was a perfectly natural mistake."

Jayne sat up straight as the television news continued, telling the world about her kidnapping. "No," she said in a tone of voice he imagined she was accustomed to having obeyed.

Boone smiled. "No?"

"Darryl doesn't strike me as the forgiving sort. He'll...he'll kill you."

"I won't let that happen."

She pursed her lips. "I don't like it."

"Sugar, you don't have to like it." Boone returned to the bathroom. He couldn't stand there wearing nothing but a towel and argue with her. After he towel-dried his hair, he pulled on his jeans and the new green T-shirt.

When he stepped out of the bathroom, Jayne was sitting up in bed, watching the last of the news and munching on the bag of soft chocolate-chip cookies she'd found among his purchases from the convenience store. She didn't sit in the center of the bed, but to one side, as if she expected them to share the bed as they had last night—her under the covers, him on top. That arrangement hadn't worked exactly as planned last night, and he didn't think it would work at all tonight.

Seeing him, she placed the cookies on the bedside table, used the remote to turn off the television and sat up very straight. Great. Her nipples were hard. Just what he needed.

"I want to know why," she said softly.

"Why what?"

"I want to know why you'd risk your life to go back to Darryl. Alone or with help, I don't care. Either way it's much too dangerous, and I want to know why."

Boone reached into the back pocket of his jeans and pulled out a worn wallet. He opened it, flipped his fingers past the condoms he had foolishly purchased at the convenience store and retrieved the small photograph that had been folded and stuck beneath a flap of leather. He tossed it to Jayne. It landed in her lap and she picked it up.

When she saw the picture, she smiled. "Cute kid. How old is he?" Her smile faded. "And what does he have to do with the case you're on?"

"He is the case." Boone circled the bed and pulled up one of the chairs they'd used for their poor excuse for dinner. He spun the chair around and sat, resting his arms across the back. "Andrew Patterson. He'll be four in a couple of months. That picture was taken more than six months ago, so he's probably changed a little."

"I don't understand." Jayne lifted those wide green eyes of hers. "Is he yours?"

"No."

"Then…"

"Erin Patterson was seventeen when she found herself pregnant. She'd been in and out of trouble for years, and she and her parents had always butted heads. But this was the last straw. They had a fight and she left."

Jayne turned her eyes to the picture. Boone didn't need to look; he had memorized that kid's face. Dark hair, dark eyes, fat cheeks and the biggest smile you could imagine.

"Erin's parents didn't hear from her for years. They

hired private investigators to find her, they…regretted their harsh words only hours after the confrontation was over. But they couldn't take those words back, and they didn't find their daughter.''

Jayne rubbed her arms with her hands as if to ward off a chill.

''Six months ago they got a letter in the mail. A letter from Erin. That picture was inside, and Erin told them she wanted to come home but was afraid she couldn't. She told them she had to sneak the letter out, that she'd become involved with a man named Joaquin Gurza, and he didn't want to let her go.''

''Oh, Boone…'' Jayne said softly.

''Three weeks later Erin's body was found in Flagstaff. She was dead from an overdose, and no one wanted to hear from two grief-stricken parents that their daughter had been murdered, that their grandson was out there somewhere in the hands of a killer. They raised a stink and they were determined to stay here in Arizona until they found Andrew. One day they had a delivery to their hotel room. Another picture of Andrew, very much like that one. The note that came with the picture warned them that if they didn't back off, the kid would be next. It also warned that if they went to the police, he would know.''

''They went home and hired you,'' Jayne said.

''Yes.''

''And you're not giving up until you find that child.''

''No.''

Jayne scooted to the end of the bed and handed him the photograph. ''I understand. But that doesn't mean you can't bring in someone to help you. My father knows—''

''No,'' Boone snapped. ''This is my fight. I bring in

anyone official, word gets to Gurza, and the kid is as
good as dead. Besides—'' he gave Jayne a crooked grin
''—no one official will even admit that Gurza exists.
They think he's some mythical bad man that lowlifes
in the Southwest use to blame for crimes they commit-
ted. The drug dealer's invisible friend.''

''But—''

''There are no photographs of the man, no official
records of any kind. We have the letter of an undisputed
troublemaker who died of an overdose, and myth. The
only real lead I have is his association with Darryl.''

''I'm so sorry,'' Jayne said, settling down there on
the end of the bed. ''This disaster is all my fault, and I
can see that finding Andrew is important to you.'' She
reached out and stroked his cheek. ''I'm sorry.'' She
knelt there, wearing nothing but that damn T-shirt, and
looked at him with big green eyes, still stroking his
cheek.

When he'd come to the door tonight bearing strawberry wine and cookies and cheese in a can, he'd been
stunned to see Jayne standing there wearing nothing but
one of his T-shirts. Beneath it, he knew she was naked.
He knew, because he still had her panties and bra in his
pocket.

He'd seen her dressed that way before; he'd seen her
wearing less. But somewhere along the way everything
had changed.

He grabbed her wrist and pulled her hand away from
his face. ''Jayne, sugar,'' he said quietly, glad of an
opportunity to change the subject, ''are you a virgin?''

''Ummm, well, kind of,'' Jayne said softly.

Boone shook his head and placed her hand on her
knee before releasing it. ''Sugar, when it comes to vir-

ginity there is no 'kind of.' The answer is yes or no.
I'm thinking the answer is yes, which is too bad—''

"No," she interrupted.

That stopped him.

"The answer is *no.*"

Jayne knew she really should have left well enough
alone, crawled beneath the covers and gone to sleep. Or
at least pretended to. Right now, tired as she was, she
probably couldn't sleep if her life depended on it.

Boone didn't look convinced. "Why the 'kind of'?"

Again, the most prudent route was probably some
kind of denial. But Jayne had taken the prudent route
all her life, and the events of the past two days had her
questioning everything about the way she lived. If not
for Boone Sinclair, she might very well be dead now.
"It was only once," she said softly. "And...and..."

"And what?" he said impatiently.

Jayne took a deep breath. If she was ever going to
be brave, now was the time. "No one's ever made me
go yee-haw." She felt a blush rising to her cheeks, but
she pushed away the childish urge to pull the covers
over her head and try to take back what she'd said. "No
one's ever made me feel like I'm close to losing control,
like I'm missing something important in my life. Not
like this," she confessed softly. "It's more than that,"
she added quickly. "No one's ever wanted me just for
me."

"I find that so hard to believe." Bless his heart, he
sounded as if he meant it.

"I was engaged for a little while," she said. "Turns
out my fiancé was more in love with Daddy's political
connections than he was with me."

"Moron," he growled.

"I've never known anyone like you," Jayne said sin-

cerely. "You're…different. Sorry," she said, mortified
that she had said so much. Terrified that Boone would
laugh at her.

He didn't. As she backed away and returned to the
safety of her place on the bed, covers all around, he left
his chair and followed her. "I like you," he said as he
sat on the bed beside her. His fingers touched her neck,
gentle, easy, undemanding fingers that caressed. "But
let's face it, you and I have nothing in common. Nothing except something physical. Maybe it's because I had
to pretend to make love to you, or maybe it's because
I've been carrying your panties around in my pocket all
day."

Jayne's heart thudded. She craved more of Boone's
tender touch in a way she had never craved anything
before.

"Maybe it's the way you screamed when you thought
of snakes." He leaned slightly forward. "I won't lie to
you, sugar. I like you, and I want you bad, but tomorrow
morning I'm going back to my world and you're going
back to yours, and we'll never see each other again. I
would love to spend the night right here. I'd like to hear
you scream yee-haw for real, but I won't pretend there's
anything more than that going on."

She took a deep breath. "What you're saying is, you
want this to be a one-night stand. You want to cavort
in bed all night and then walk away in the morning with
no ties, no promises to call me or get together for dinner
when this is all over. All you want is the sex."

"Yeah. Right now I'm wound so tight I'm about to
explode. You are, too, you just don't realize it yet." He
laid his hand over her breast, brushed a thumb over an
already hard nipple. "We're just talking about blowing
off steam here. That's all."

She knew that if she indignantly rejected his offer, Boone would back off and they'd never speak of it again. Maybe that was what he expected. Maybe that was what she should do. She was so tired of always doing what she should. For once, just for once, she wanted to take what she craved without thinking about tomorrow.

Jayne fisted her hand in Boone's shirt and pulled him gently toward her. "Okay."

He seemed surprised for half a second, and then he kissed her. His mouth molded to hers, he forced her lips apart with his and kissed her deeply. His tongue slipped into her mouth, teased her with flutters and swirls while his fingers teased her breasts the same way.

Heat pooled low in her belly, and her breath caught in her throat, low and fluttery.

Boone kissed the way he did everything else. Thoroughly. Expertly. He kissed her until she could think of nothing else but the way his body felt against hers, the way his wicked mouth made her toes curl.

He slipped his hand beneath her shirt and raked it over her bare skin, over her belly, up her torso to touch her breasts and roll the nipples gently between his fingers. Sensations, gentle and not so gentle, billowed through her body.

With a steady hand at her back, Boone brought her into a sitting position. He pulled the T-shirt over her head and tossed it aside. No man had ever seen her like this, completely naked and vulnerable, trembling with something she didn't completely understand. Maybe this was just one night of many for Boone, but it was an important night for her. One that would never come again. She offered him more than her body; she offered him her trust and a newly discovered piece of her heart.

He touched her, his big hands surprisingly gentle and arousing. His kiss she knew, but the touching was different. So beautifully real and tender. His mouth left hers and teased her throat…rousing an unexpectedly strong sensation that made her quiver deep. When Boone brought his mouth to her breasts, first one, then the other, a jolt of pure sensation washed through her. He kissed and suckled until her bones turned to butter and her core throbbed with need.

It was much too late for anything resembling second thoughts. Everything she was, she trusted into Boone's hands. She felt safe here, safe and wanted and aroused beyond imagination.

When Boone's hands trembled, she sighed. He needed her as much as she needed him, and she liked that.

"You," she said, reaching out to take his shirt in her hands. "Why are you still dressed?"

"What's your hurry?" he teased, but he lifted his arms so she could yank the dark-green shirt over his head.

Heavens, she loved the sight of his chest. Hard, muscled, light sprinkling of dark hair, so different from her own. She laid her hands on him and teased his small flat nipples. While she touched and explored, Boone kissed and nibbled her shoulder, then her neck.

They fell back, his hard chest pressing against her soft breasts, his arms bracketing and protecting her. And he kissed her mouth again.

She understood now what Boone meant when he said he was about to explode. Her body, too, was nearing eruption.

While he kissed her, she reached down and touched him. Denim covered his erection, but she could feel it with her curious fingers. The length, the hardness, the heat. She raked her fingers up and down, and Boone answered with a long low growl of a moan.

Now. Surely he would enter her now. But he didn't. Instead, he backed away a little, placed his hands on the insides of her thighs and spread her legs wide. His hands caressed her thighs, up and down and up again. And then he touched her. With gentle fingers, he caressed her intimately. Her hips surged to meet his caress.

He kissed her again while he touched her, and something wonderful danced just out of reach. Jayne rocked against his hand, threaded her fingers through his hair and held on tight as she returned his kiss fiercely.

And then he was gone. She felt as though something she needed, the way she needed air to breathe, had been snatched away. But Boone wasn't gone. He removed his jeans, ripped open the foil condom package and sheathed himself. And then he was on top of her again. Her arms wrapped around his neck, her legs wrapped around his hips. And he guided himself into her.

He stretched and filled her, moving slowly, entering her with tender power. When he was all the way inside her, deep and complete, he held himself there and Jayne held her breath. It was unexpectedly beautiful, breathtakingly exciting.

Boone began to move, shaking the bed with his thrusts. The headboard banged against the wall, and then again and again. Jayne rocked with him.

His thrusts were slow at first, long strokes that made her moan and rise to meet him. His speed increased. The bed squeaked, the headboard banged, and Jayne couldn't stop the low moans that escaped from her throat.

Sensations she had not known were possible shimmied and jolted through her; a depth of need she had not expected made her reach for him in every way. The passion wasn't hers or his, it was *theirs,* and it was potent.

Boone drove deep and she shattered, crying out with the force of her completion, then holding on tight as the waves washed over her. He came with her, while her muscles milked and stroked his length. Strong tremors worked through his body as he caught her up tightly and groaned. He even whispered her name, before he shuddered one last time and lowered himself to cover her, still at last.

Jayne wound her fingers through his hair and held him close. She couldn't breathe deep, and her entire body trembled. Her heart pounded, she was covered with sweat...and she was wonderfully, deliriously happy.

Words she knew she couldn't possibly mean teased her lips. *I love you.* It was an emotional reaction to a memorable moment, and if she let the words slip out, Boone would be horrified. He hadn't come to her looking for love. Still, she couldn't deny what she felt.

It wasn't gratitude for everything he'd done for her; it wasn't simply physical. Perhaps it wasn't love, but that was the only word she could put to the emotion that flowed through her.

Boone lifted his head and grinned down at her. "Damn," he said softly.

Jayne brushed back a long strand of hair and whispered, "Yee-haw."

Chapter 8

Boone rolled onto his side and pulled Jayne closer to him. She murmured in her sleep before settling comfortably against his chest.

He had not expected the elegant lady who chastised him for cursing, averted her eyes when she caught him in his boxers and readily admitted to being "kind of" a virgin to let loose the way she had. Jayne had taken him by surprise, first by her acceptance of his less-than-romantic offer of one night and then by her unbridled response. These days Boone didn't let anything surprise him.

If she wasn't exactly the wrong kind of woman for him, he might think about calling on Jayne when this was all over. What a crock. He didn't *call on* anyone, and besides, her father the senator would have heart failure if Boone Sinclair came courtin'.

No, this was it. All they had was tonight, and one night would have to be enough.

He wasn't going to waste it sleeping, though.

He placed his hand on Jayne's hip and moved his fingers over her backside. The glow from the bathroom cast just enough light across the bed for him to admire her fair skin, those perfectly feminine curves and valleys, and a small birthmark on one rounded cheek, a couple of inches beneath her waist. His fingers traced the tiny mark, and Jayne stirred. Just a little.

His hand moved downward, brushing the back of her thigh, cupping the inside of her knee. His fingers fluttered there, teasing her. Waking her slowly.

She came awake with a sigh and a leisurely undulation, and her arm draped around his waist. Her fingers gently stroked his spine. For a few minutes they lay just that way, touching tenderly and savoring the heat they generated. And they did generate some heat.

Boone rolled Jayne onto her back. Her breasts rose and fell as she breathed deep, and he skimmed his fingers across the curve of one, then over a nipple, which peaked at his touch.

Jayne smiled sleepily. He had never known a woman who could smile that way, sweet and wicked at the same time. She so openly and completely responded to his every touch. Each sensation was new to her, each a ribbon of pleasure she had never known before. He heard wonder in the catches of her breath, in the way she whispered his name.

He skimmed his hand down and rested his palm against her belly, then leaned over to lick the skin around her belly button, his tongue circling and teasing. Jayne answered with a deep tremor and a sigh that was almost a moan.

She wasn't at all the kind of woman he'd thought she was, with her pearls and her proper language and her expensive shoes. She had a hidden steely resolve, a good heart, and in bed…in bed she was open and trusting and giving. Which absolutely bewildered him. At least for tonight, he could fool himself that her passion was his, that he was the only man who would ever make her moan and writhe this way.

When he touched her inner thigh, she parted her legs slightly. When he stroked her, she parted those thighs more. All he had to do was touch her and she was ready. He could bury himself inside her now, and she'd climax in a heartbeat.

Too soon.

When he lowered his head between her thighs and placed his mouth on her, Jayne shuddered and almost came off the bed.

If tonight was all they had, he wanted her to have everything. He wanted her to walk out of here in the morning with no regrets. Hell, he wanted her to glow for weeks; he wanted her to think about him and smile every night for the next month. Or two. Or forever.

His tongue circled and teased lightly, barely touching her at first. When she rested her hands in his hair and began to move against him, he stroked her harder. Faster. Longer. She came quick and hard, arching her back, moaning and quivering while he tasted her response.

He had never wanted to be inside a woman as much as he wanted to be in Jayne. Now. He climbed up slowly, hovered above her. She wrapped her arms around his neck and gave him one of those special smiles. With a gentle nudge, she urged him onto his back.

"What a wonderful way to wake up," she whispered, leaning over him to press her mouth against his neck. Her lips were soft and warm, and she sucked gently at his neck while her hands settled on his chest. "You feel so good." She raked her palm down his chest to his belly. "I just want to touch you all over."

"Go ahead."

Jayne's hands, tentative at first and then bold, examined him. She took her time, lingering over his hips, watching as her hands caressed and aroused him. She traced her fingers down his thighs and teased the backs of his knees.

As arousing as the way she touched him was the expression on her face. The wonder of an unexplored pleasure was there, in the parting of her lips, in every tilt of her head.

Soft hands trailed slowly up his inner thighs, and Jayne's fingers very lightly brushed over his erection. Kneeling beside him, she wrapped her fingers around his length, studying him, stroking him.

Unable to take this torture any longer, Boone reached for the bedside table and grabbed a rubber. He ripped the foil package open, and Jayne very nimbly took the condom from him.

"Let me," she whispered.

For a moment she studied the condom as she had studied him, and then, using both hands, she covered him with the sheath. A woman like this one could make a man crazy, Boone decided.

Jayne started to roll away onto her back, but Boone stopped her. He held her atop him, adjusted her leg so that she straddled him, and then he guided himself to her.

She smiled as she moved her hips slightly, teasing him with the slow progression of their joining. Boone closed his eyes as Jayne's tight body made way for him. An inch at a time.

When he opened his eyes, Jayne was no longer smiling. The desire he could see in her eyes matched his own; the parting of her lips was intoxicating. She lifted her body and descended again, taking more of him.

She rose and fell, her breasts swaying slightly, her hair falling over one cheek. He'd always thought Jayne delicate, fragile, and she was. But she was also sexy and strong. Right now she was in control, and she liked it. She didn't back away or pretend to be shy, but rode him as if she knew what she wanted and wasn't afraid to take it. Her eyes closed and her body shuddered; she was on the verge of another climax.

He'd waited as long as he could—a woman could only ask so much of a man. Boone grasped Jayne's hips in his hands and rose to meet her as she descended. He thrust farther into her than he'd been before, and that was all it took to send her over the edge. She trembled, cried out softly, and as she shuddered and moaned, he joined her, climaxing hard.

Jayne drifted down to him, kissed his mouth lazily, laid her head against his shoulder. "Oh, my," she said breathlessly.

Boone threaded his fingers through her red-gold curls and held her tightly. This one night was not going to be nearly long enough.

When Jayne awoke next, it was early morning. Too early to be up, considering how little sleep she'd gotten.

As she had been most of the night, she was caught against Boone's chest. Not a bad place to be. She was safe here, in more ways than one. No one would hurt her, not while she was here. And Boone…Boone didn't expect her to be anyone or anything she didn't want to be. She was more than safe. In his arms, she was free.

She reveled in the feel of his body against hers, and it was more than the sex that made her adore this closeness. It was so basic, the need to be close to another human being. To hold and to protect and to cherish. When she'd first seen him, she never would have believed that Boone Sinclair would be the one to make her understand that.

"Why aren't you asleep?" he growled, his breath warm in her ear.

"I'm worried," she said truthfully.

"About what?"

"About you." She tilted her head back so she could see his stubbled, harsh, beautiful face. "I don't want you to go back to Darryl's."

"Sugar—"

"And if you have to go, if there's really no other way, please don't go alone. Please."

He was quiet for a few minutes, but she knew he hadn't gone back to sleep. "It's what I do," he said softly, his hand moving gently in her hair. "I…find lost children. I take them home. I'm not leaving Arizona without Andrew."

His dedication made her own life seem so meaningless. She spoke to women's clubs, attended teas, worked with her father in a strictly social capacity, when Lucille Barrington had another engagement or could not be persuaded to leave Mississippi and the home she loved. There was some charity work, but Jayne had never been as passionate about any cause as Boone was about finding Andrew Patterson.

"Fine," she murmured. "At least bring in some backup. Get someone to help you. A lot of someones would be even better."

"Don't worry about me," he said, his voice low. "I'll be fine."

She wished she could believe that, but she didn't. Boone was reckless, and a dedicated man who was also reckless was bound to put himself in danger. "I can talk to my father. The local authorities might not want to believe that Gurza exists, but we can convince him. I know we can."

Boone raised himself on one elbow and looked down at her. "I don't want anything from your father. I don't want his help, I don't want him to pull any strings for me. I don't want him to call in the National Guard."

"He could do all those things."

"Yeah, and if word got out, the kid would be in serious trouble. Let me handle this on my own, sugar."

She wrinkled her nose, annoyed. "All right, BooBoo, but I don't like it. I don't like it at all."

He grinned. "Cute. I have to warn you, if you ever call me BooBoo in front of anyone over the age of six months, there will be serious repercussions."

"What kind of repercussions?"

"You don't want to know," he said ominously, and then he settled back down beside her, gathered her into his embrace and stroked her back. "Go to sleep, Jayne."

She cuddled against his chest, buried her nose there and took a long deep breath. She loved the way he smelled. It was the way a man was supposed to smell—clean and musky, warm and smoky. He smelled of leather and soap. And her. "Boone?"

"Mmm."

"You won't ever have to worry about me calling you BooBoo in front of anyone over the age of six months,

because after today we won't see each other again.''
Her heart hitched. "Right?"

"Right," he answered sleepily.

Jayne lay there, warm and worried and confused.
Boone had no problem falling back to sleep. His arms
relaxed, his breathing became deep and even.

In a matter of days her entire life had changed. *She*
had changed. How was she supposed to go back without
missing this? No man would ever again hold her quite
this way, not even if she did manage to find one who
didn't want her for her father's political connections,
even if she did find a man one day who made her shake
and shudder the way Boone did. Even if all that happened…it wouldn't be like this. She knew it.

She tried to tell herself that she felt this way because
Boone was—in every sense that mattered—her first.
The fact that he had saved her life, that he was her
guardian angel, her knight in tarnished armor, only
made what she was feeling for him now more intense.

How could he sleep so well, knowing that come
morning they'd head their separate ways?

"I'm going to miss you," she confessed, her voice a
whisper. "I don't think I'm ever going to meet anyone
like you, not ever again." She brushed her cheek
against his chest and closed her eyes. "Heaven help me,
I think I could love you."

Fully dressed and wide awake, Boone leaned over a
sleeping Jayne. "Wake up," he said for the third time.
Finally deciding that a word or two was not going to
do the trick, he slapped her on her bare bottom.

That did it. Jayne sat up quickly, grabbing the sheet
that was twisted around her and pulling it to her chest.
Her eyes were wide, her cheeks deliciously pink. That

one exposed leg—delicate foot to shapely calf to sweet knee to even sweeter thigh—was tempting. With a little persuasion he might be convinced to delay their parting for a few more minutes.

But he couldn't do that, no matter how much he wanted to. He'd promised Jayne one night and they'd had it. And what a night it had been. She'd had her yee-haw and he'd been amazed in a way he had not expected. But today it was back to business for both of them. Besides, Dean would be here in less than half an hour.

"Get up and get dressed, unless you want to meet my big brother wearing nothing but a smile."

"Your brother?" Jayne scrambled off the bed, modestly taking the sheet with her. Still wrapping the sheet around her, or trying to, she stooped to snag the T-shirt he'd peeled off her and tossed aside last night.

"He's a deputy U.S. marshal. The *good* brother," he added. "Dean's going to escort you back to Flagstaff."

Jayne glanced over her shoulder as she stepped into the bathroom. "I thought you were going to do that."

Did she really sound disappointed? Or was that his imagination?

"No. I'll ride with you most of the way, but I can't go all the way to your hotel. It would be best if we weren't seen together. As a matter of fact—" he moved closer to the bathroom door "—I'd like to ask you to do me a favor."

Jayne stepped from the bathroom, wearing only that pale-blue T-shirt. "Anything," she said.

"Keep a low profile for a few days. Don't answer the reporters' questions, don't give any interviews. Most of all, don't mention my name. Either of them."

She pursed her lips. "Because you're going back."

"Yeah."

His insistence on continuing with this case made her angry. Her cheeks flushed and her lips thinned. "You are the most stubborn man I've ever met."

"Thank you."

Her hands balled into tiny fists. "Are you at least going to get some help?"

Boone shrugged, took his eyes off Jayne and reached for his weapon, sticking it into the waistband of his jeans. "Maybe."

Jayne lifted her hand slowly and wagged her finger. "Aren't you afraid you'll...shoot off your favorite body part?"

He grinned. "Safety's on."

"Oh." Without further argument she collected her suit and returned to the bathroom, closing the door behind her this time.

Just a minute later, the door opened a crack and Jayne's arm shot out. "You have my, um, underwear in your jacket." How could she sound even the tiniest bit embarrassed after last night?

Boone reached into his pocket and withdrew the bra and panties. They were silk, tiny little slips of satiny material. With lace. He offered the ultrafeminine garments at the end of an outstretched arm, and Jayne quickly snagged them.

With the bathroom door firmly shut on him once again, Boone paced the motel room and ran his fingers through his hair.

"All that matters is the job," he muttered. "Not some witchy woman, not the itch in my pants, just the *job.*"

"Did you say something?" Jayne called.

"No," he said curtly.

His eyes bored into the bathroom door. Why did he have this awful nagging feeling that putting Jayne Barrington out of his mind was going to be the hardest thing he'd ever done?

Chapter 9

Deputy U.S. Marshal Dean Sinclair was very much like his brother Boone in some ways. They both had dark-brown hair, a sharp jawline and stood six foot. Both had the wide Sinclair smile. But Dean wore a suit and a conservative haircut, and his eyes were blue, not brown. And she could not imagine Dean Sinclair ever trekking across the wilderness with some woman's panties in his pocket. He was much too dignified.

He reminded Jayne, just a little bit, of the men who had pursued her in the past. Clean-cut, all-American straight-arrows. In as many ways as they were alike, he and Boone were very different.

Her father would most likely adore Dean Sinclair.

They rode toward Flagstaff, she and Dean in the front seat, Boone in the back. He had insisted on riding there, even though Jayne had suggested, more than once, that he sit up front with his brother. She wished she'd been more persistent. This way she couldn't see Boone at all unless she turned her head, and she couldn't very well endure the long drive to Flagstaff in that contorted position.

Boone must've filled his brother in by phone last night. While Dean had a few questions, he seemed very much up to speed. There wasn't nearly enough conversation to make the miles go by faster.

Boone stuck his hand into the front seat. "Do you have a pen?"

Dean reached into his shirt pocket and blindly handed a pen back.

While Boone scribbled away, Dean glanced at Jayne and smiled softly. "Are you really okay? Sounds like you've been through quite an ordeal."

"I'm fine," she said demurely, fiddling with the pearls at her throat as they sped toward Flagstaff. "It was an ordeal, but it would have been much much worse if Boone hadn't been there."

She would not have survived if Boone hadn't been there. She would be dead now if Boone hadn't been there.

Boone handed the pen back over the seat, and Dean took it, returning the pen to its place in his pocket.

Last night she had accepted the fact that when tomorrow came, she and Boone would part company. Tomorrow had arrived, the parting was imminent, and her stomach was tied in knots. She wasn't ready. She would likely never be ready to say goodbye.

All she could do was pretend it didn't hurt so that when Boone remembered her, the memories would be only good ones.

As they neared the city, Boone leaned forward and gave Dean directions. Not to Jayne's hotel, but to the place where he was to meet with his DEA cohorts.

Jayne had met plenty of federal agents in her day. Most of them were cookie-cutter copies of Dean: dark suit, conservative tie, determined jaw. How could men like that go up against Darryl?

With every minute that passed, Jayne became more and more anxious. This was it. Boone was going to get out of the car and walk away and she'd never see him again. They didn't have any choice. She didn't fit in his world and he didn't fit in hers. Still, she hated the very thought of the coming goodbye.

Boone pointed to a corner up ahead, where two long-haired thugs stood, smoking and laughing. One was tall, black-haired and wide-shouldered, and wearing a black leather jacket. The other man was smaller, thin, blond and scraggly-looking.

"Maybe you should go to another corner," Jayne suggested softly.

Dean ignored her and pulled up to the curb. Boone threw open the back door as the car was coming to a stop. The two thugs approached.

Jayne's heart jumped into her throat, and she rolled down her window quickly. "Boone," she said, her hand on the door handle. Heavens, he was jumping right back into the fire!

She couldn't open the door, because Boone placed himself in a position to block her. "These gentlemen are Agents Wilder and Shockley," he said softly. "Take it easy."

Take it easy. How on earth was she supposed to take anything easy! The three of them standing there together looked like every mother's worst nightmare.

"Didn't anyone ever tell you that long hair is no longer in fashion?" she snapped.

Boone's eyebrows shot up. "Oh, no. I didn't get the

memo.'' The two DEA agents were standing too close behind Boone. He turned to glance at the dark-haired one. ''Wilder, did you get the memo about long hair being out of style?''

''Nope. I musta been on vacation that week.''

The little man with the stringy pale hair spoke up, his voice whiny. ''They never tell me anything. I think we should sue. How *embarrassing*.''

Jayne felt herself blushing. She'd spent most of her life making sure she knew exactly what to say and what not to say. She never got flustered and said the wrong thing, but where Boone was concerned, all bets were off. This was no way to say goodbye.

''Sorry,'' she said. ''I just...thank you.''

He grinned, that wonderful Boone grin, and offered his hand for a proper handshake. ''Any time, Miss Barrington.'' The handshake was quick, professional, cold. When it was done, he handed her a business card. ''If you ever need a P.I., give me a call.''

Jayne's heart dropped to her knees. *Miss Barrington? If you ever need a P.I.?* ''Good luck,'' she said softly, but it was too late. Boone had already turned away and was talking to his two long-haired buddies, and Dean pulled the car away from the curb.

Jayne stared out the window as Dean drove toward the hotel in silence. Well, what had she expected? To Boone, last night was just a chance to blow off a little steam. Sex without strings. That was exactly what he'd offered her, and she'd accepted without a second thought.

She could have been anyone. In a week he wouldn't even remember her name. A couple of tears she refused to shed burned her eyes. Damn him and his business card. She glanced down at the plain white card. ''Boone

Sinclair, private investigator. Specializing in finding lost children.'' There was a phone number, a cell phone number and a Birmingham, Alabama, address.

She considered wadding the card into a ball and tossing it, but instead, found herself playing with the business card the way she sometimes played with her pearls. Once, when she flicked the card between two fingers, she caught a glimpse of blue ink on the back side of the card. She flipped the card over.

''You're amazing,'' it read. ''If you ever need anything, call me.''

Jayne folded her fingers over the card. *Amazing.* No one had ever called her amazing before. She looked out on the passing city streets and smiled.

Over coffee in an out-of-the-way café not far from where Dean had dropped him off, Boone told Del and Shock everything they needed to know about what had happened and what was to come. No more. As far as they were concerned, Jayne was simply a complication. She was Miss Barrington the senator's daughter, who'd just happened to wind up where she didn't belong. She was a hands-off kind of woman, and she was out of their league. True enough.

''I would love to bring in Gurza,'' Shock said. ''Man, that would be like putting handcuffs on the bogeyman.'' The little guy was a bit too excited, which was normal for him.

Del was more skeptical. ''There's still no concrete proof. A single letter, a few ramblings by criminals looking to put the blame on someone else...''

''A missing kid,'' Boone added.

Del shrugged. ''I'm not making light of the situation, but the kid's your problem, not ours.''

Boone leaned back in his seat. He liked Del, and he even liked Shock. He trusted them both, which was why they were here, instead of the agents who normally worked this jurisdiction. Like him, Del and Shock were based out of Birmingham.

And he was still tempted to walk out of here and finish the job on his own. But he kept hearing Jayne's urgent *Please* in the dark. ''All I want you to do is get Darryl and his boys out of the way for a few days,'' he said. ''I have everything you need to arrest them and then some. A quick raid, you toss them in jail, and they're out of my hair.''

''We'll have to bring the locals in,'' Del said.

''Then do it.''

Del took a long swallow of coffee. When he set his mug on the table, he directed his curious eyes at Boone. ''The senator's daughter looks like she can be a real pain in the ass.''

''Uh-huh,'' Boone mumbled.

''Pretty enough, though,'' he added with a smile. ''For that type.''

Boone couldn't help himself. ''What type is that?'' Immediately he knew he shouldn't have asked. Wilder was having way too much fun with this.

''The type that'll take you to a dinner where they give you twelve forks, and you're supposed to know which one to eat what with.'' Del's eyes positively twinkled.

''Oh, man, I hate it when that happens,'' Shock grumbled.

Del wasn't finished. ''The type that always looks like a proper lady, even when she's wearing a T-shirt with some stupid saying on the front.''

That was Jayne, Boone conceded silently.

Del's grin widened. "The type that, when she gets pissed off, instead of telling you what she really thinks, tells you your hairstyle is out of fashion."

"That type," Boone said tightly.

Del laughed. "You are in so much trouble."

"Can we just stick to business?" Boone snapped.

Shock leaned over the table and grinned. "When you're finished with Gurza, can we have him? Pretty please?"

Boone stood and tossed a bill onto the table. "If there's anything left, he's all yours."

Jayne leaned back in the tub and closed her eyes. The water was so hot it steamed and turned her skin pink. This was heavenly.

It had taken her much too long to get to the tub. She'd honored Boone's request and steered clear of the media. It hadn't been easy. Dean had helped her with the necessary short interview with the police. He'd quickly gotten rid of the much-too-interested police and sheriff's deputies with the edict that this was a federal case. The locals had persisted, but when Dean had stared them down and given them a no-nonsense "Miss Barrington will not be answering any more of your questions tonight," they'd backed off. Maybe Dean had more in common with his little brother Boone than was immediately apparent.

The hotel was now screening Jayne's phone calls for her, after she'd had to handle a few on her own, and security had cleared the hallway of reporters at her insistent request. As soon as she'd found herself alone, she went straight to the phone. The ensuing conversations—with her father in D.C., then her mother and grandmother in Mississippi and then her father again—

had been long and a little tearful. All had gone well, until her father had insisted that she return home immediately. She'd told him she wasn't ready, and when he'd questioned her, she'd said she wanted to spend a week in bed.

It was the truth. Problem was, she didn't want to spend that week alone....

Her father had threatened to fly out and collect her, but she'd asked him not to, first citing that he was needed in D.C., then telling him that she wanted to be alone for a while.

Just as the water began to cool, a sharp knock sounded on her door. Jayne smiled as she left the tub and grabbed the large terry-cloth hotel robe from a handy bathroom hook. *Boone.* She belted the robe tightly as she ran to answer the knock. When she peeked through the peephole, though, she was sorely disappointed.

"Pamela," she said as she opened the door. "Come in."

Pamela gave Jayne an overly dramatic hug before continuing into the room.

Her hotel room in Flagstaff was nothing like the motel where she and Boone had stayed last night. This room was actually a suite, with a large bathroom, a living room complete with sofa, tables, a desk, two fat chairs and a small bar, and a plushly carpeted bedroom. The king-size bed was adorned with half-a-dozen fat pillows.

It was elegant and extravagant, and right now it was also very lonely.

"Thank God you're all right!" Pamela said as she walked to the couch and collapsed. "You sounded fine on the phone, but I just had to see for myself."

"I'm doing great, all things considered," Jayne said, curling up in a chair and tucking her feet beneath her.

"You look tired," Pamela said kindly.

"I am."

She couldn't tell anyone about Boone, not ever. Pamela was her friend, but she wouldn't understand. She certainly couldn't tell her mother. Everyone else… everyone else was likely to sell the story to some journalist who would make a stink that might damage her father's political career—and Boone's business, too. He was her secret, her deepest, darkest, most wonderful secret.

"Jim is anxious to see you," Pamela said with a huge smile. "He said we should come by his apartment tonight. He can't really get out since he's still recuperating."

Jayne's heart sank. Jim was recuperating from a scratch and a fainting spell, to hear Boone tell it. "I can't."

Pamela's smile died. "But Jim was so certain that you two, you know, were really hitting it off before…the incident."

Telling Pamela that Jim was a moron wasn't going to help matters any. "I just can't see him without being reminded of what happened," she explained. "Right now I don't think I could handle that."

Pamela nodded, and her eyes went hard. "Jayne, did they hurt you?" she asked.

"No," Jayne said quickly, giving her friend a smile of assurance. "I was just scared for a while, that's all."

"How did you get away?"

Jayne wanted to trust Pamela, she really did, but she didn't trust anyone with this. If word got out, Boone might be in danger. He was in enough trouble as it was.

"I really don't want to talk about it," she said. "Not now. I'm here and fine and that's all that matters."

"You're right," Pamela said, nodding. "Nothing else matters. Come to dinner tomorrow night," she said. "I'll make that Shrimp Divine you like so much."

Jayne was tempted to say yes, just to have something to do, something to take her mind off Boone. Why did she have the sinking feeling that Jim would show up before dessert? "I'd better not. I need a few more days."

Jayne settled back and let her friend do most of the talking. Pamela talked about how brave Jim was— *gag*—and then she started talking about her family. This was the part of the conversation Jayne enjoyed. She snuggled beneath the terry robe and listened as Pamela raved about her kids. A boy and a girl, four and two years old, respectively. They were beautiful, they were smart, and most of all they were filled with unconditional love. Pamela's husband, his friendship with Jim aside, seemed to be a really good guy. He was, after all, baby-sitting tonight while Pamela checked on her friend.

Jayne wanted all that—the unconditional love especially. The problem was, until she'd met Boone, every relationship or potential relationship had come with too many strings attached. Boone was the only man she'd ever met who didn't look at her and see a political connection. He looked at her and saw a woman, and for that she would always love him, a little.

When she walked Pamela to the door and said goodnight, Jayne wondered, with a shiver, where Boone was at that moment. When the phone rang, she couldn't help but wonder, *Is it him?* She ran to answer.

* * *

Boone stood on the opposite side of the road in shadow, while Del, Shock and a contingent of locals stormed the shack. It was almost dawn, a good time to catch the dealers asleep and unprepared.

It wouldn't do for any of the men in that shack to see Boone—their Richard Becker—with the cops. No matter what Jayne said, this wasn't over. It couldn't be. He didn't have the time to go up against Darryl and the boys, and this house-cleaning would mean starting over, dammit. But what choice did he have?

Waiting was hell. Especially since while he waited, he kept thinking about Jayne. He wasn't supposed to think about her. She was over, done, one night he should be able to dismiss without a second thought. If her memory lingered, it was because she was different from the other women he'd known, that was all.

Minutes passed, minutes that ticked by too slowly. He had to consider the possibility that Darryl had gotten smart and cleared out, along with the stash of drugs Boone had told the DEA agents was there.

Finally the sheriff's deputies led out two handcuffed, squalling young men. Doug and Marty did not go easily or quietly.

Another deputy followed, gingerly carrying a bag of evidence. Drugs, probably. If that small bag was it, then Darryl had managed to get most of the stuff out.

A few minutes later, Del came to the door of the shack and gave Boone the high sign. Apparently Darryl was not at home this morning. Boone cursed as he headed for the side door.

"Not much," Del said as Boone approached. "But enough to hold those two for a while. If they'll give us Darryl, maybe we can—"

"They won't," Boone said. If nothing else, the boys were terrified of Darryl. And rightly so.

What a mess. Darryl had left the boys here as what— bait? A test to see if they were raided? Maybe he'd convinced Doug and Marty that Jayne wouldn't be able to provide decent directions to the shack, and that Becker wouldn't. No man who valued his hide would go up against Darryl and Gurza.

He entered the familiar kitchen and then walked into the living room. Nothing had changed in a day. Nothing except the addition of Darryl's new television, which sat on the TV stand, bright and shiny and stolen. The local cops would have to see about finding the rightful owner.

Boone stopped and raked his fingers through his hair. Now what? Without Darryl he had nothing on Gurza. Absolutely nothing. He hadn't been kidding when he'd told Jayne that he'd start over if he had to. But how? With Darryl out there somewhere, starting over became much more dangerous.

He didn't have any choice.

From the back of the house, Shock whined, "You guys better come look at this."

Boone ran, following the sound of Shock's tinny voice. The agent had called from the bedroom that had been Boone's for a few harrowing weeks. Wilder was right behind him.

When Boone walked into the room and found Shock standing over the bed, his heart lurched. When he followed the agent's gaze to the mattress, his vision blurred and his stomach rolled.

A small, satiny piece of lingerie—Jayne's slip—had been sliced in two and tossed across the end of the bed. Her blouse, the one they'd left behind because it had

Chapter 10

No wonder Jim had gotten lost on his way to Corbin Marsh's vacation home. The town car Jayne rode in now had made several turns, and presently they drove down a narrow highway that wound through the middle of nowhere. The road was bracketed on either side by wide plains, red rocks and scruffy little bushes. Already they were more than an hour out of Flagstaff.

It had been her idea to have Marsh's driver pick her up at the hotel at a very early hour. She wanted to avoid running into reporters who might be waiting in the lobby, and an early getaway seemed like a good idea. The driver, a solidly built man with very little neck and even less hair who looked like he was five pounds away from bursting out of his uniform, had introduced himself as Harvey. Harvey didn't talk much.

The call from Marsh inviting her to spend a few days at his isolated home had been just what she needed last night. Well, if it couldn't have been Boone on the phone, this was the next best thing. No reporters, no Jim, no big empty hotel room. She could turn her mind back to the business that had brought her to Arizona—drumming up support for her father—and get her mind off of a long-haired foul-mouthed bully who just happened to be a gorgeous hunk of a man and a fabulous lover.

It should be easy to dismiss Boone as a meaningless one-night stand, but she couldn't. Like it or not, he meant something to her and always would. Somehow she had to get past that. She had to put him out of her mind once and for all. Why was that so difficult?

She couldn't say she believed in love at first sight, and she'd definitely not fallen in love with Boone when she'd first laid eyes on him. She'd been terrified. But even then, she'd known he was the one she could rely on to protect her. Her instincts hadn't failed her completely. When had she known he was really and truly different? That she felt something more than gratitude for him?

Jayne knew, without a doubt, when that moment had come. She'd jumped, and he'd caught her. She'd leaped from a cliff ledge, trusting that Boone would catch her. Her life had been in his hands, and she had felt safe. Somehow she knew that Boone would always catch her when she fell. Not always, she amended sadly. They didn't have always.

Exhausted, she napped in the car, resting her head against the seat and dozing fitfully. When she opened her eyes, the car was on the slightly winding approach to a sprawling Spanish-style house. She couldn't help but smile. It was a lovely place and suited the landscape surrounding it. The stucco walls were a very pale pink, the plants that grew along the borders of the house were typical of this part of the country—jagged and tough. The house was at once elegant and simple, if you could call a U-shaped home that was surely seven or eight thousand square feet "simple."

The town car pulled around the circular driveway to let Jayne out at the front door. Before she could step from the car, the double front doors opened, and Corbin Marsh met her with a gleaming smile.

"Miss Barrington," he said as he practically danced toward her. His loose-fitting beige pants and the sleeves of a matching shirt swayed as he approached. "I'm so happy you decided to accept my hospitality."

Jayne offered her hand for a shake. It was quickly sandwiched between both of Marsh's eager hands. "Jayne," she said.

Marsh gave her another dazzling smile. "Delighted." He lifted her hand and pressed a kiss to the knuckles.

Jayne was accustomed to men who tried to dazzle her with charm, but Marsh was in a league all his own. According to his bio, he was forty-five, but he could pass for ten years younger. His pale-brown hair was just a little bit long, covering his ears and almost touching his collar, and his eyes were an interesting pale blue. He had a quick, utterly enchanting smile that brought out the laugh lines around his eyes. His clothes were downright baggy, and still he looked like a man who worked out regularly. Something about the way he held himself and the strength in his hands.

He was handsome enough, she supposed. He might have been a movie star, instead of a producer. The only feature on his face that was less than perfect was his nose, which was just a little too long and narrow.

She'd been expecting someone like her father, she supposed, since Marsh was only five years younger than the senator from Mississippi. Maybe agreeing to stay here hadn't been such a good idea....

Nonsense. Corbin Marsh was interested in supporting her father politically, nothing more.

He led her into the house while Harvey collected her bags from the trunk.

"I want you to relax while you're a guest in my home," Marsh said. "I feel just terrible that you experienced such trouble while you were on your way here. I should have sent a car for you that night. If I had, you wouldn't have found yourself in such a predicament."

"What happened is certainly not your fault," she said. Jim had been the one to insist that he could drive her to Marsh's and back. Moron.

Harvey, who had no trouble carrying her three bags, came into the house and closed the door behind him. Marsh glanced over his shoulder. "The blue room in the north wing," he instructed. The driver nodded and carried the bags off.

Marsh took Jayne's arm and guided her through the foyer, into the hallway where Harvey had carried her bags and onward. They walked down a long hallway that ended in a large dining room, lit by sunlight streaming through a floor-to-ceiling window. It was a warm welcoming room, not at all imposing as many formal dining rooms were.

"You must be hungry," Marsh said, pulling out a chair for her. "Benita has prepared breakfast for us."

"Lovely," Jayne said, not at all hungry but not wanting to be rude.

Benita must have been waiting for them to arrive. She walked into the room no more than two minutes after Jayne took her seat, bearing two large platters of food.

Each platter held a Southwest omelette and an assortment of breads—a muffin, a biscuit, thick toast. Whatever she might prefer was there. Another younger girl was right behind Benita, with cups of coffee and glasses of juice.

Jayne smiled and nodded at the two women, who responded with nods of their own, eyes downcast. Benita was obviously of Mexican descent, a middle-aged woman who did not smile. The other girl was blond and green-eyed and very pretty. She didn't smile, either.

"You certainly do know how to make a guest feel welcome, Mr. Marsh," Jayne said as she sampled her omelette. "This is wonderful."

"Corbin," he said as he dug into his own breakfast. "Only actors and directors call me Mr. Marsh."

Jayne gave him her best political smile.

"And I do want to hear about everything that happened," he added. "Who knows? Your adventure might make an excellent film."

Jayne almost choked on her biscuit. "I hardly think so," she said when she'd recovered.

"Well," he prompted, "what happened?"

Jayne took a deep breath. She'd have to continue to tell the story she'd used to pacify the police last night. "I was kidnapped briefly. Locked in a horrid little room in a horrid little house, and when the criminals weren't looking, I ran."

"You just…ran," he said.

Jayne nodded. "I caught them off guard, I think."

"You're a brave girl," Corbin said, flashing his Hollywood smile.

She didn't bother to tell him that she didn't feel at all brave.

*   *   *

"What do you mean she's not here!" Boone shouted. He leaned over the front desk, and the manager of the hotel—Kyle Norton, according to the gold name tag on his pocket—leaned sharply back.

"Miss Barrington is not in, I assure you," the pale man repeated.

Behind him, Del and Shock waited. At the news that Jayne was not in, Shock mumbled something obscene.

Boone took a deep breath. Calm. He needed to remain calm. It had been bad enough when the operator had refused to put his call through to Jayne's room. A sheriff's deputy running interference had finally gotten him through…and no one had answered the damn phone. Of course no one had answered. Jayne was doing exactly as he'd asked her. She was avoiding the press. "She told you to say that, I understand. But this is important!"

Del stepped forward and flashed his badge. "It's extremely urgent that we speak to Miss Barrington," he said calmly.

Norton studied Del's badge. "She's not here, I swear it. She checked out very early this morning."

"Checked out?" Boone shouted. His heart dropped to his knees. "Was she alone?" he asked in a lower voice. Please, please, let her be alone. If the manager told them Jayne had left this hotel in the company of a very large man—

"Yes," Norton said. "She left alone. A car met her out front."

"And you didn't ask her where she was going?" Boone reached over the counter and grabbed Norton's shirtfront. The alarmed man looked to Del for help…and got none.

"It's not my concern where our guests go when they

leave us," Norton said, his voice almost calm, his Adam's apple working up and down.

"A car met her," Del said, leaning on the desk beside Boone and the trapped manager. "Did you recognize the driver?"

"No."

"Did Miss Barrington seem alarmed at all or nervous?" Del continued.

"No," Norton said quickly. "She seemed...a little tired, that's all."

Del offered his large hand to the manager, palm up. "We'll need the key to her room."

Norton glanced warily at Boone. "It's over there," he said, pointing to the opposite end of the desk.

Boone released Norton abruptly, and the man almost fell over backward. A half second later Norton was back with a key card. "It'll still work. I haven't rekeyed the lock yet. Room 1012."

The three of them made their way to the elevators, walking quickly, their strides long. People got out of their way, parting cooperatively as Boone, Del and Shock walked past. Maybe it was because they were moving with such purpose.

Maybe people moved aside because not one of the three of them looked like this hotel's usual guests. Then again, maybe it was because they were all armed.

They had the elevator to themselves. "We'll check the airports first," Del said calmly. "She probably just decided to catch an early flight and go home. I'll have someone call the senator to check on that possibility."

"She didn't fly out," Boone said.

"How do you know?" Shock asked.

"The itch in the middle of my back, that's how I know." Neither of them would argue with him on that

point. You heeded your instincts when you worked the
kinds of jobs they did. You didn't ignore the itch in the
middle of your back.

Jayne's room was neat and offered no clue as to
where she might have gone. No notes by the phone,
nothing in the wastebasket. Boone stalked through the
hotel suite, wanting very badly to break something.
Anything. He didn't.

Something unexpected happened as he moved
around. He felt Jayne here. Sensed her, smelled her.
Some deeply hidden part of himself came to life, went
on alert. She was his, and dammit, she had a way of
finding trouble.

The bed was hardly mussed. Jayne had climbed in,
tucked herself beneath the covers and slept without
moving an inch. This bed didn't look at all like the one
they'd shared, covers ripped off and tossed aside, sheets
twisted.

He caught a glimpse of something blue beneath the
covers and reached out to snag the T-shirt he'd bought
her at the convenience store. Had she forgotten it? Or
left it behind on purpose? She'd probably left it here
for the maids to dispose of. A T-shirt from a convenience store was definitely not Jayne's style.

"Okay," Del said sensibly. "Airports first, just in
case. You want to call her father?"

"Hell, no," Boone muttered as he fisted his hand
around the T-shirt.

"Dean still around?" Shock asked as he wandered
into the bedroom.

"He was planning to fly out this afternoon, but he'll
stick around if I ask him to."

"We could call in help…" Del began.

"No. If this is connected to Gurza in any way, stirring things up will only put Jayne in danger.'' More danger than she was already in, dammit.

Shock grumbled, ''So the four of us are supposed to go after a legendary bad guy we don't even know where to start looking for?''

Boone didn't trust anyone else. He certainly wasn't going to trust a local cop who might very well be in Gurza's pocket. A man didn't stay invisible this long without a little help.

''Five,'' he muttered. ''I have another brother.''

A quiet day at Corbin Marsh's home was just what she needed, Jayne decided as she stepped into the court-yard after a long afternoon nap. Corbin had excused himself to take care of some pressing business, leaving her to relax. He'd offered the use of his library, Benita's assistance in fetching anything she might desire and the most exquisite room she'd ever stayed in.

The blue room where Harvey had carried her things was large and square and decorated in varying shades of blue that should not have worked but somehow did. The furniture was simple but elegant, the fabrics lush and expensive. The effect was soothing. The room had a king-size bed, its own bathroom—including a whirl-pool—a television and a pair of wonderfully fat chairs that sat by the window overlooking the courtyard.

At the center of the courtyard, where Jayne had de-cided to spend the afternoon, a fountain sparkled and sprayed and gurgled. The patio floor was of red tile, and so many tall, well-cared-for plants filled the courtyard it seemed completely isolated, even though it was bracketed on three sides by the pink stucco house. The fourth side of the square opened onto a vast and empty prairie she could barely see through the lush growth and the ornate wrought-iron fence.

For the afternoon she'd changed into a pale yellow sundress and a pair of simple white sandals. If she was going to relax here, she might as well *really* relax. Before she got on with her life, she needed to find herself again. She needed to decide who she wanted to be.

Boone knew exactly who he was. She envied him that. He had a purpose—finding his lost children—and never wavered from it. He was open and honest and, yes, occasionally crude.

Everything *she* was and had been for years was tied up in her father. Her family. She had nothing that was truly her own, and until she'd met Boone that hadn't bothered her. Now she wondered who she was, who she could be.

Marsh joined her, Benita right behind bearing two tall glasses of iced tea and a plate of homemade cookies.

"It is lovely, isn't it?" he asked, his smile bright.

"Yes," Jayne agreed. "Enchanting."

She needed to remember that she was here to drum up support for her father. Corbin Marsh represented a lot to a politician with hopes of moving onward and upward. He had money of course, but more than that he had connections to Hollywood, where actors and famous directors sometimes tended to be vocal about their political beliefs.

Jayne felt a small uneasy butterfly take flight in her stomach. Being a senator's daughter was tough enough. If her father did one day run for president and he actually won, her position would be much more public than it was now. Sure, she had years before she had to worry, but still…she did worry.

Marsh handed her a glass of tea, which she gratefully

accepted. "Why is such a beautiful young woman like you spending the weekend at my house all alone?" he asked, sounding a little puzzled. "You should have many suitors trailing after you."

She gave him a polite smile.

"This Jim who was going to bring you to the party, the young fellow who was wounded, are you two—" Corbin gave his free hand a little suggestive wave "—involved?"

"Heavens, no," Jayne said sharply. "Jim is just a friend of a friend. I barely know him."

"There must be someone," Corbin continued with a sly smile.

Jayne started to deny the implication, but she felt the heat of a blush rise to her cheeks.

"I see I've gone too far," Corbin said. "Forgive me for being rude. I just can't imagine such a beautiful woman all alone."

She didn't really think he was making a pass at her, but with Marsh it was difficult to tell. "I'm not exactly all alone," she said.

"I'm glad to hear it," he said, "and not surprised. I'm afraid your blush gave you away. It's so refreshing to meet a woman who doesn't lie as if it's second nature."

Jayne was trying to come up with a proper response, something not offensive that would, nonetheless, defend her gender, when a new sound drifted to the courtyard. She could swear it was a child's laughter.

Marsh heard it, too, and turned toward the courtyard doors that stood wide open. "I believe you are about to meet my nephew."

"I didn't even know you had a nephew," Jayne said with a smile. "Does he live with you?"

"Yes. Drew's mother was my sister. She passed away a few months ago and I've had him with me ever since."

"How sad," Jayne said, "about your sister."

Marsh shrugged off her concern, but didn't look her in the eye. "My little sister was always a bit of a problem. Wild. Reckless. Drew is the only thing of value she ever produced."

His words were harsh for a loving brother, but perhaps he was still angry about her death.

The laughter came closer and was accompanied by the sound of small feet pounding on the tile floor. "Drew!" an exasperated female voice called. A babysitter? A nanny? She couldn't see Corbin Marsh taking on the care of a child, so she imagined it was a nanny who chased Drew through the house.

Marsh turned to meet his nephew as the boy flew through the open doors. The producer crouched down and offered his arms, and the child flew into them. An exasperated young woman with pale-brown hair and a lean face stopped in the doorway.

"What did you learn today?" Marsh asked, eyes on his nephew.

Jayne heard a small voice respond, "I learned the B sound and the C sound and we watched a movie."

"Was it a good movie?"

"Yes! It was about dragons."

With a wave of his hand, Marsh dismissed the nanny. The young woman withdrew.

Corbin turned around with the child in his arms. "Drew, we have a guest, and I want you to be especially good while she's here."

"'Kay," the boy said.

Jayne saw dark hair first, then a full cheek, and when

the child turned to smile at her, she almost dropped her glass of tea. After the harrowing events of the past several days, she knew better than to give herself away. She didn't jump or scream or mutter, ''Oh, my God.'' She didn't run or faint or tremble. She hoped to high heaven she didn't turn too pale.

''This is Miss Barrington,'' Marsh said.

Jayne touched Drew's cheek with tender fingers. His skin was so soft, so delicate and fragile. ''Miss Barrington is a mouthful. How about plain old Jayne?''

''Miss Jayne, then,'' Marsh said as he shifted the boy in his arms. ''I want Drew to grow up with some proper manners. Say hello to Miss Jayne, Drew.''

''Hello, Miss Jayne,'' the boy said shyly.

''Hello, Drew,'' she said. ''I'm very pleased to meet you.''

Jayne's heart hammered. Her mouth went dry. The boy Marsh said was his nephew was the child in the picture Boone had shown her. There was no doubt in her mind.

Drew was Andrew Patterson.

Chapter 11

Doug and Marty weren't talking. At all. Jayne Barrington hadn't been on any flight out of Flagstaff that day—no surprise to Boone—and a deputy U.S marshal calling to ask the senator from Mississippi if he'd heard from his daughter that day had only managed to rile the man up again.

Every minute that passed without news, Boone's insides wound a little more tightly. Had he thought that once he had her away from the shack, this was over? Stupid. He should have known Darryl wouldn't just let Jayne walk away. He should have known there would be a price to pay for his arrogance and his rash decisions. There always was.

Darryl was in with Gurza, and Gurza had no qualms about killing people who got in his way. Boone couldn't help but think of Erin Patterson, who had ended up shot full of drugs and left to die on a dead-end street. Darryl wouldn't have a second thought about doing the same thing to Jayne, no matter who she was.

Del and Shock were hitting all the bars and pool halls Boone had visited during his time in Arizona. These were Darryl's hangouts, his places of business. Right now the agents were undercover as potential customers. If someone blew their cover, Doug and Marty would take the blame.

Boone's brother Clint had recently arrived at the hotel after catching an early-afternoon plane from his home in northern Alabama. Norton, the cooperative hotel manager, had given the three brothers two connecting rooms. Anything to get Boone away from his front desk.

Boone sat on the edge of one bed, staring at the floor, while Dean stood at the window and Clint paced. Why was it the only time they got together was for holidays and when there was trouble?

"Okay," the youngest Sinclair brother said, "I think I got it. Except for one thing. Why are *we* looking for this chick, instead of some…I don't know, Navy SEALs or commandos or something?"

Boone lifted his head and glared at Clint.

"Oh," Clint drawled, deciphering Boone's look quickly. "I *see*."

"You see nothing," Boone growled. "I got her into trouble, I'm getting her out."

"Fair enough," Clint said, unconvinced but not pushing the issue. Clint never pushed the issue. He was one of the most laid-back men Boone had ever met. Sometimes he wondered if they were really related by blood.

"Once Del and Shock get a lead on Darryl, we move in. Quick and hard—there's no other way." He waited for the cell phone on his hip to ring. He waited for Del and Shock to come through with…something. Anything.

He had a really bad feeling that Jayne wouldn't make it through the night without him.

Jayne waited, knowing that to rush to the telephone so soon after meeting Drew would be a mistake. She waited. An hour. Two. Using the excuse that the nights got cool and she needed a sweater, Jayne went into the blue bedroom, took her purse from the bottom dresser drawer and grabbed Boone's business card, dropping it into the pocket of her yellow sundress before slipping on a lightweight white cardigan.

And then she waited some more. She and Corbin talked about films he'd produced, books they'd read and Drew. They talked a lot about Drew. Jayne kept trying to come up with some explanation for Corbin's lie that he was Drew's uncle, some rationalization. He seemed to truly care about the little boy. Was he working for the man Boone searched for? Were they even, perhaps, partners? She wanted to believe that there was an innocent explanation for the boy's presence here, but she couldn't come up with one.

Finally Marsh excused himself to make some urgent business calls from his office. Jayne stopped him as he was leaving the room. ''When you're finished, would you mind if I borrowed your phone? I really should call my father.''

''Of course.'' Corbin directed her to the phone in the library, which he said was on a different line from the one in his office, and when he left the room he closed the door behind him—but not quite all the way. It hung open a couple of inches.

Instead of taking the card from her pocket, Jayne di-

aled her father's office number, his private line, praying
he would still be in at this hour. He usually was. He
answered the phone with a gruff, "Hello."

"Daddy?" Jayne said.

"Jayne! For goodness' sake, where are you? I've
been worried sick. I had a phone call—"

"I'm fine," she interrupted. "I decided to spend a
few days at Corbin Marsh's house. He invited me here,
and I thought maybe I could finish the job I came to
Arizona to do."

There was a moment of silence. When her father took
these long pauses, it was not a good sign. He was col-
lecting his thoughts, trying to come up with a calm and
rational response. "And you didn't think to tell anyone
where you were going?"

"I called Pamela last night and told her where I'd
be," Jayne explained.

"Oh, yes," her father said softly, "Pamela. I should
have called her, but I did assume that if you were going
to check out of the hotel, you'd let me or your mother
know where you were going." His voice grew tighter
with every word.

"Sorry," she said. "With everything that's happened, I'm not thinking clearly. I didn't mean to worry
you." It had been late last night when Marsh had called,
and she'd left the hotel so early.

There was a moment of awkward silence. "Jayne,"
her father finally said, his voice deepening, "are you at
that house with Marsh...unchaperoned?"

She couldn't help but smile. "Hardly. His nephew
lives here, and so far I've met four live-in servants. I'm
sure there are more."

Out of the corner of her eye, she saw the library door

open. Corbin Marsh stuck his head in and smiled. Jayne looked up as he walked in.

"Do you think I could say hello to the senator?" he asked as he approached. "We've spoken on the phone a few times, but it's been a while. I'd like to assure him that his little girl is in good hands."

"Of course," Jayne said. "Daddy, Mr. Marsh would like to say hello."

The men held a brief cordial conversation, which ended with an invitation for the senator and his wife to vacation at the Arizona house. When that was done, Corbin handed her the phone and left so she could say goodbye in private.

"Daddy?" Jayne said as the library door swung almost closed. She wondered how much, if anything, she could tell him. If he knew she was putting herself in the middle of something sticky, if not dangerous, he would insist that she leave immediately. When she refused, he'd send in the army to get her out. In the end she just said, "I love you."

"I love you, too, sweetheart."

Jayne hung up, took Boone's card from her pocket and dialed. It only rang once before he answered with a harsh, "Sinclair."

"Boone?" she said softly, her eyes on the library door.

"Jayne! Where are you? I've been half out of my mind with worry." He muttered a foul word, and she didn't even try to chastise him.

"Listen to me. The boy is here. Andrew Patterson is *here.*"

There was a moment of silence before Boone asked, "Sugar, where are you?"

"I'm at Corbin Marsh's house, where Jim and I were

headed that night.'' She lowered her voice further.
"Marsh says Andrew is his nephew.''

"Okay,'' Boone said, his voice low and calm. "You
get out of there. Now.''

"No.''

"Make some excuse,'' he said. "And get out of that
house *now*.''

"No,'' she said again.

"What do you mean, no?'' he shouted.

Jayne kept her eyes riveted on the door, worried that
Marsh would return, anxiously waiting for a servant to
check on her. That was what Marsh had been doing,
she knew, asking to speak to her father. He'd been
checking up on her story. That was not the action of an
innocent man. "I'm not leaving here without that
child,'' she whispered.

"Jayne.'' She could tell that Boone was struggling to
reason with her, that he was fighting a growing anger.
"Walk out of there while you still can. I'll get the boy.
I promise.''

"I'm not running away and leaving Drew behind.''

A despairing sigh drifted to her across the phone
lines.

"Don't argue with me,'' she said, not giving him a
chance to do so. "You wouldn't run.''

"That's different.''

"I don't see how.''

"You're getting in the way again,'' he said testily.
"All you have to do is walk out the front door and I'll
have *one* child to rescue, instead of *two!*''

Indignation rose within her. "Are you calling me a
child?'' Her voice rose slightly. "How dare you? Oh,
you make me insane, do you know that? You make

me…'' A shift of light in the hallway caught her eye. Someone was out there. Marsh again?

"Jayne?" Boone snapped, obviously alarmed by her sudden silence.

"You just make me crazy," she said in a softer voice.

"I'll be there as soon as I can, dammit," he said. "Be careful. Promise me that."

The door swung open and once again Marsh walked in. How much had he heard? Not everything, but probably enough to know she was no longer talking to her father.

"I hope you don't mind," she said, moving her mouth away from the phone and smiling at Marsh. "I needed to make one more phone call."

He nodded politely. "My home is your home. This is the boyfriend you refused to talk about this afternoon?" The question was accompanied by a smile.

"Jayne," Boone said quietly, "is that him?"

"Yes," Jayne said, her answer directed to both men.

"Is he in Arizona?" Marsh asked.

Jayne nodded.

"Then you must invite him to join us for the weekend. I hate the idea of such a beautiful woman suffering because she is separated from the one she…loves?" His eyebrows rose slightly in question.

"Jayne, dammit, talk to me," Boone said softly.

"That's very sweet of you." Jayne moved her mouth closer to the phone. "Honey, Mr. Marsh has invited you to join us for the weekend."

"Great," Boone growled. "I'll be right there. Where the hell are you, exactly?"

"Stubborn pigheaded, witchy woman," Boone muttered as he stared out the window. The deserted landscape was dark, lit only by the headlights of Dean's rental car and the off-center headlights of the dilapidated truck Clint drove behind them. "She should be out of there by now."

"So you've told me several times," Dean said calmly.

"Speed it up," Boone said. "You're driving like an old woman."

Dean glanced at the speedometer. "I am not. This is why I didn't let you drive," he added.

"Let me?" Boone snapped, taking his anxiety out on his older brother.

"Yeah." Dean shifted in his seat as if he was getting a little uncomfortable. "Don't be too hard on her for staying. You'd do the same thing if you were in her shoes."

"Entirely different circumstance, and you know it," Boone said sharply. "Jayne is just going to foul things up." She would place herself in danger and take his mind off the job. "Now I have two people to recover, instead of one."

"She's getting you inside the house," Dean reasoned. "That should be worth something."

Boone grumbled an indecipherable response.

Dean laughed. "You must really like her."

Boone started to deny it, then shrugged and said, "She's all right."

"All right?"

"Maybe a little more than all right," Boone conceded.

"You remember to keep your head on straight in there," Dean said, his voice low and deadly serious. "Don't get distracted."

"Who, me?"

Dean had been watching out for all of them for as long as Boone could remember. Not that their parents hadn't loved them. They'd just been so wrapped up in their own lives they'd often let things slide. Like birthdays or dinner or those lectures most kids got from their parents. Boone, Clint and their sister, Shea, had gotten those lectures from Dean, along with the occasional meal of peanut-butter sandwiches. Oh, their father was really big on grand talks about justice and doing what was right, which was probably why Dean and Boone had both ended up in law enforcement. But Dean had been the one to take care of them. In the end, they had learned to take care of one another.

"How much time are you going to need?" Dean asked.

"I don't know. I do not want y'all to come in with guns blazing while Jayne and the kid are there. Let me see if I can get them out without anyone getting hurt."

"If the kid was really kidnapped, it's not going to be that easy."

Boone stared at the passing rugged terrain. "I know. I'll need a day, maybe two."

"We'll be close by, and you have three ways to signal us. When the time comes, you should be able to do at least one."

They reached a crossroads and pulled off onto the shoulder. Clint pulled in behind them. As Boone left Dean's rental car, Clint tossed him the keys to the truck. He didn't get a lecture from Clint, just a quiet "Good luck."

Jayne heard the vehicle long before it rumbled to a stop at the front door. The noise was impossible to miss.

Something sputtered. When the car door opened it squealed.

She knew it was Boone. Still, when the doorbell rang, she nearly came out of her chair. Corbin noticed and smiled as he rose to his feet. "Anxious to see this boyfriend of yours?"

She nodded. Corbin hadn't even asked her for a name, which was a good thing. Who would Boone be today? Boone Sinclair, P.I.? Richard Becker, goon? Or someone else entirely?

She followed Corbin to the foyer and was standing behind him when he opened the door.

Oh, this was not good. Boone did not look happy, and he had that pistol stuck in his waistband. She found herself hoping he'd remembered to put the safety on. If they made it to Christmas, she was buying him a shoulder holster.

Boone's eyes traveled past Corbin to find her, and visible relief washed over his face. "Sugar," he said as Corbin opened the door wide and Boone stepped into the house.

"BooBoo," she said softly.

He cocked his head and narrowed one eye. Well, what was she supposed to call him when she didn't have any idea who he was today? He looked bigger than ever, meaner, tougher with a day's stubble and that long hair. And she had never been so happy to see anyone in her life.

Boone walked past Corbin without giving the man more than a cursory greeting, his eyes never leaving her. "Still mad at me?" he asked softly.

"Just a little," she said, and then she rose on tiptoe to meet him for a kiss. The kiss was sweet and tender, until he took her lower lip between his teeth and bit her! It was a gentle nip, true, but she had a feeling it was an admonishment all the same.

When Boone took his mouth from hers, giving her one last meaningful glare, he smiled at Corbin and offered his hand.

"Boone Sinclair," he said. "Thanks for inviting me."

"Corbin Marsh," their host said, shaking Boone's hand and studying him with a trace of amusement in his pale eyes. "Glad to have you, though I must say you are not quite what I expected."

Boone grinned. "I guess not."

Corbin pointed at the pistol Boone carried. "I will have to ask you to hand that over. I have a great aversion to guns. Don't allow them in the house." He lifted a hand, and Harvey appeared without making a sound. "Harvey, put Mr. Sinclair's weapon in the safe, please. We're all friends here."

Jayne wondered what would happen if Boone refused to hand over his pistol. For a long silent moment, they all waited.

Boone reluctantly handed over the pistol.

"When the gun is safely locked away, collect Mr. Sinclair's luggage from his vehicle." Corbin nodded to Boone. "I assume you do have luggage."

"Sure."

"Put him in the green room." Nodding once, Harvey—gun in hand—made a quiet exit.

"Do you have a permit for that weapon, Mr. Sinclair?"

An unsmiling Boone stared pointedly at Corbin. "Uh, yeah."

Marsh looked amused, and Jayne couldn't blame him. No one who knew her would accept Boone as her boyfriend. And he wasn't. He was her lover, or had been. He was her friend, and if she had her way, he always would be. But they were as different as night and day, and Marsh saw that.

Jayne wrapped her arm through Boone's. "Corbin insisted that we hold dinner for you. Are you hungry?"

"Does a bear—"

"Boone!"

"Yeah," he said. "I'm starving."

Corbin led the way to the dining room. "Does the senator know about you, Boone?" he asked, glancing back briefly.

"Nope," Boone said. "Not yet, anyway."

"I think I may have to ease Daddy gently into the idea of Boone," Jayne said, squeezing his arm gently.

Corbin laughed. "I can certainly understand that."

Boone wrapped his arm around her…and grabbed a bit of flesh on her side to give it a gentle tweak. She squealed, just a little, and Marsh looked back.

"Stop that," she hissed at Boone.

He just smiled.

Chapter 12

He couldn't figure out exactly how or why Corbin Marsh was connected to Joaquin Gurza, but somehow it was true. Boone kicked back on the elegant white sofa in Marsh's living room, nursing a beer while Marsh and Jayne each enjoyed a glass of wine. She finally got her damned Merlot.

Jayne sat next to him, close but not too close, nervous but not so much so that her behavior was in any way odd. And every now and then she did something unexpected, like laying her hand on his knee or glancing at him and biting her lower lip. Jayne Barrington was a great actress. If Marsh wasn't obviously crooked, Boone might have suggested that she audition for a part in one of his movies.

Every now and then Boone caught Marsh looking at him in a very calculating way. Because the idea of Jayne Barrington and Boone Sinclair together was so ludicrous? Or because he suspected something more than an absurd romance was at play here?

Boone heard the kid coming long before he saw the little boy walk in, his hand held by a thin young woman. The child appeared freshly bathed and was dressed in colorful pajamas. Boone's breath hitched. It was definitely Andrew Patterson.

Marsh smiled and waved the little boy into the room. The young woman waited silently in the arched doorway.

"All ready for bed, I see," Marsh said as Andrew skipped toward him. "Aren't you up a little late tonight?"

"I was watching a movie," the boy explained.

"Another one? That makes two today."

"Miss Lacey said I could," Andrew said, glancing toward the doorway.

Marsh looked at Jayne briefly and gave her what seemed to be a proud smile. "The child loves movies, as long as there's lots of music and action. I'm afraid even the most scintillating dialogue puts him straight to sleep, but I'm sure that in time he'll come to appreciate the finer details. One day he'll be a fine director."

Boone watched while Andrew climbed onto Marsh's knee and gave the man a kiss on the cheek. His insides tightened. This was not exactly what he'd expected to find. "G'night, Unca Corbin."

"Tell Miss Jayne good-night," Marsh instructed softly, and Andrew climbed off his "uncle's" lap and crossed to the sofa.

"G'night, Miss Jayne," he said softly, his eyes flickering anxiously to Boone. Great. The kid loved the bad guy and was afraid of the man who had come here to rescue him. This would not be easy.

"Good night, Drew," Jayne said with a smile. "Can I have a kiss, too?"

The boy moved nearer, carefully avoiding coming too close to Boone. His size sometimes scared kids, he knew, that and the hair. And maybe the scowl.

Drew climbed onto Jayne's lap and kissed her on the cheek. She didn't let the kid go right away, but wrapped her arms around his cartoon-pajamaed waist and turned her head to the side, resting her smooth cheek against the boy's. "Drew, this is my very good friend, Boone. You can call him Uncle BooBoo."

Drew brought a little hand to his mouth and giggled.

"I know," Jayne said softly. "It's a funny name, isn't it?"

Drew nodded, and his eyes landed firmly and without fear on Boone's face.

Jayne stroked her hand down the child's back, cuddled him a little, and something in Boone went bump. They made quite a picture, Jayne in her yellow sundress and white sweater and with her red-gold curls, Drew with his big brown eyes and bare feet. Someday Jayne would have kids of her own, and she would hold them just this way...

"Tell our guests good-night, Drew," Marsh instructed. "You've had a long day."

"Don't I get a kiss, too?" Boone asked with a smile.

Drew shook his head, but he did grin as he scrambled down off Jayne's lap. "G'night, Unca BooBoo," the boy said as he ran off, giggling.

Boone directed his gaze at Jayne. "Even a small child knows BooBoo is...ridiculous."

She leaned slightly toward him. "I think it's cute."

Boone sighed, resisting the urge to reach out and grab Jayne and kiss her the way she needed to be kissed.

Hard and deep. He wanted to thank her somehow. At this rate the kid wouldn't be afraid of him for long. Who could be afraid of a man who allowed people to call him BooBoo?

Jayne set her half-finished glass of wine aside and rose to her feet. "I've had a long day myself," she said. "I really need to get to bed."

Boone stood, intent on walking Jayne to her room. Marsh stopped him.

"Please stay a few moments longer, Boone," he said formally. "We barely know one another, and I'd like to get better acquainted with you. Just the two of us."

Jayne rose on her toes and Boone kissed her briefly. "I'm in the north wing, third door on the left," she whispered.

Marsh probably overheard, but of course he would think Jayne was giving Boone directions to her room for a different reason from the practical one she no doubt had in mind.

When Jayne was gone, Marsh's smile faded and Boone reclaimed his seat on the white sofa.

"So what do you do?" Marsh asked bluntly. "I assume you have a job of some kind."

If Gurza had the kind of connections Boone suspected he had, lying would only get him in trouble. He'd have to choose his lies carefully. "I'm a private investigator."

Eyebrows came up. "Here in Arizona?"

"I work out of Birmingham, Alabama."

"Is that how you met Jayne? Through your work?"

Boone cocked his head to one side. "No," he said simply.

"Might I ask how you did meet?"

"Just one of those things," Boone said with a shrug.

Marsh opened his mouth to continue, but Boone beat him to the punch. "What's next? Are you going to ask me if my intentions are honorable? If you are, let me save you some time. None of your damned business."

Marsh leaned back in his chair, very smug in his loose beige outfit and sandals. He looked like some kind of hippie who had been sucked into a time warp. "I don't buy it," he said.

Boone's heart skipped a beat. "You don't buy what?"

"You and her—it doesn't quite work. I know people. Yes, the chemistry is there, but I know character and motivation, and you two as a couple doesn't feel right. What are you really—private security? Do you work for the senator?"

Boone grinned. "Hell no, I don't work for the senator. Do you need proof before I can follow my woman to bed? You want some kind of concrete evidence that we're really involved? Fine. She has a birthmark on her ass. It's shaped like the state of Florida, but only if you look at it upside down." He made a square using both hands and tilted it sharply. "Like that."

Marsh's smile faded quickly. "Crude and interesting, but difficult to verify."

"Ask her if she has a birthmark," Boone said nonchalantly. "She won't answer, but she will most definitely blush."

Marsh settled back in his chair and studied Boone like a bug under a microscope. Apparently he was still not convinced. "What do you see in her? A man like you, I'd think you'd go for a more…earthy type."

Boone's smile faded. "Don't you have eyes? What's not to like? Jayne's beautiful, she's warm, she's… good." The truth. No lies to be dissected by this man or Gurza. "Do you know how few really good people there are in the world? I'm talking about deep-down honest and fair. Jayne doesn't do what's right because it's expected of her, she does it because it's who she is. I don't know a lot of really good people." His jaw tightened. So far he hadn't said a word that wasn't true. "Beyond that, what I see in her is—once again—none of your business." His eyes went hard. "Are you asking all these questions because you have plans for Jayne yourself?"

"Of course not," Marsh answered indignantly.

"You'd better not," Boone said. "She's mine. You so much as look at her in a way I don't like, and I will kick your ass right before I haul her out of here."

Marsh relaxed visibly. He'd bought it, for now, Boone thought. "Well, they do say opposites attract. Perhaps you two are living proof of it."

Boone unfolded his body from the couch and stood, hoping that if he showed any eagerness to follow Jayne, Marsh would think it was for more *earthy* reasons than the real one.

He was going to kill her.

Jayne answered the soft knock, throwing the door back and all but dragging Boone into the room. He closed the door behind him and dropped his duffel bag onto the floor.

"What are we going to—"

Boone grabbed her wrist and pulled her hard against his chest, then kissed her. She knew this kiss. It was of the "shut up" variety.

Slowly he took his mouth from hers. Before she had a chance to speak again, he placed a silencing finger over his lips.

His eyes scanned the room. He was looking for something.

"You run in interesting circles, sugar," he said as he began to search the room. He went down on his knees and ran his hands over the underside of the table nearest the door. "This is some fancy place."

"Yes," she said, immediately understanding what he was doing. But why would Corbin Marsh have his guest rooms bugged? Then again, why would he claim that Andrew Patterson was his nephew? "I'm glad you came," she added in a softer voice.

"Like you could keep me away."

He continued his search as they carried on their conversation. Jayne twiddled her thumbs. What could she safely say? They could hardly talk about the weather.

"I was afraid you might be mad at me," she said softly. "You know, after the things we said last time we saw each other."

He smiled crookedly. "So, should I cut my hair?" He got down on the floor and spent several long seconds looking under the bed.

"No," Jayne said as Boone stood and went to the window, running his hands around the frame. "I like it, fashionable or not. It suits you." She couldn't imagine Boone in a suit, his hair cut short and his manner dignified. She liked him just as he was. Wild and unrestrained and noble.

He continued to search the room, looking in the smallest crevices and around every piece of furniture. "I noticed that you left the T-shirt I bought you behind. No big deal," he added. "It wasn't expensive or anything. I just wondered if you were trying to say something by getting rid of it."

Her breath hitched. She'd slept in that shirt last night,

in her Flagstaff hotel, even though her own nightgowns were available. "I was a little angry, I guess," she admitted. She hadn't thought she'd ever see Boone again. Keeping remembrances would be silly. Unnecessary. Painful.

"I brought it with me," he said, his back to her.

"Good."

Boone's search was thorough, but so far he'd found nothing. "I can't believe you called me BooBoo in front of someone else," he said, shaking his head slowly. "I warned you what would happen if you ever called me by that stupid name when there was anyone over the age of six months around."

"Repercussions," she said softly.

"Exactly." Boone lay down on the floor and stared up at the underside of the bedside table. He shook his head, rolled up and pointed to his ear. Someone was listening.

"Drew was afraid of you," she said. "If you had smiled, instead of glowered, I likely would not have had to resort to the BooBoo defense."

"I don't glower," Boone said as he walked toward her.

"You're glowering now."

When he reached her, Boone bracketed her face with his hands and stared down at her. He shook his head in what might have been dismay. "You drive me crazy," he said. "Why on earth did you come all this way without even telling me where you were headed?"

"I needed to get away," she said. True enough, no matter who was listening.

"Come on." Boone dropped his hands from her face and grabbed her hand. "I need a shower." He pulled her toward the private bath, grabbing his duffel bag as they passed.

"There's no shower," she said as she followed. "Just a whirlpool bath."

"That'll do," Boone said.

When they were in the bathroom with the door closed, he quickly searched for more listening devices. He didn't find any, but was taking no chances. He sat on the side of the tub and turned the water on. With a rough hand he urged her to sit beside him, and then he leaned close and whispered in her ear.

"You should have gotten out of here when I told you to."

Jayne listed toward Boone, and kept her voice low when she answered, "I couldn't." Surely he would understand that she couldn't just walk away and leave that child. What if Marsh got suspicious about her quick departure and took the boy to another location? They might never find him again.

"Why on earth did you wear your gun out in the open?" she asked, anxious to change the subject.

"Doesn't matter where I carried it. They would have found it, anyway. Given my cover to this point, it seemed best not to hide the weapon." He glared at her. "I can't believe you didn't go when I told you to."

"Boone..."

"We'll talk about this again when we get out of here," he said. It sounded suspiciously like a warning. Since the tub was filling quickly, he turned on the water jets. More noise filled the room. "Where's the kid's room?"

"The south wing, I think."

"You don't have anything more specific?"

Jayne shook her head. "Sorry. I haven't been in that

wing. I think that's where Marsh's office and his personal rooms are, so I assume that's where Drew's room is.''

''I'll find out tomorrow.''

Her heart lurched. ''How long is this going to take?''

''A couple of days, maybe,'' Boone whispered. ''I can't come in here with my own army and shoot my way out, not with you and the kid in the way.''

Jayne laid her fingers on his shoulder. ''I'm in the way again?''

Boone hesitated before answering, ''Yes.'' And then his hand rested on her waist, possessive and warm. ''But if not for you, I'd be back to square one. Thanks.'' His jaw was tight, the muscles in his neck tense. ''I got a little worried when I couldn't find you. What were you thinking, just checking out of the hotel without telling anyone?''

''I told Pamela.''

''You should have told Dean or your father. Or…me.''

''I know,'' she said. ''Everything happened so fast. I just wanted a little time to think.''

When she'd left the hotel, they'd already said goodbye. She hadn't expected that he would want to be apprised of her movements. But then, she hadn't expected to find Drew Patterson here, either. ''You don't have to worry about me.''

''Worrying about you seems to be turning into a career,'' Boone said reluctantly.

As the water ran noisily, the moment to tell Boone that he didn't ever have to worry about her passed. The fact that he did worry seemed to baffle him. Maybe she meant more to him than he was willing to admit.

Time to change the subject. Jayne smiled. ''For a

man who specializes in finding lost children, you aren't very good with them. You really glowered at Drew.''

''I did not.''

''Did, too,'' she whispered. ''Just a little.''

Boone moved closer. His breath touched her neck. ''I usually deal with older children,'' he said. ''Runaways, for the most part.''

Jayne all but nuzzled his neck. ''Why?''

Boone drew back, turned off the water and shook his head as he brought a finger to his lips again.

''Are you going to take a bath with me, sugar?'' he asked with a wink.

''I'd better not.''

He stood and started to undress, pulling the T-shirt over his head.

Jayne averted her eyes. He was here on business, people were listening, and he'd never promised her more than one night. ''I'll get ready for bed,'' she said, turning away.

Before she could escape, Boone grabbed her around the waist and pulled her back. She thudded against his bare chest. ''You really are amazing,'' he said softly. His voice dropped to less than a whisper. ''Remember, he's listening. Be careful.''

When he left the bathroom, he found Jayne sitting up in bed. She wore a white cotton nightgown, something prim and proper and unexpectedly sexy. The woman could make a flannel shirt three sizes too big look sexy!

Her eyes were huge, and when they landed on him, he saw the fear there. And that fear reminded him that she didn't belong here. She was out of her league. And she didn't even know about Darryl's threat, the knife through her blouse. He decided then and there not to tell her. Not until they were out of here, anyway. She had enough to worry about. A hysterical Jayne would not help matters any. She was wound tight enough as it was.

And so was he.

He had, in the interest of decorum and Jayne's tender sensibilities, put on a pair of navy-blue boxers.

"You're naked," she said softly.

"Yes, I am."

She licked her bottom lip. Tilted her head slightly. "You have your own room across the hall."

Boone sat on the side of the bed. *I'm not leaving you here alone.* He didn't make a sound, but Jayne could read his lips. She nodded once.

"I'd rather stay here, with you," he said for whoever was listening.

"Okay," she said, scooting over. She didn't hide under the covers and pat the top of the bed for him, just threw them back and invited him in. "But I have a headache."

He slipped beneath the covers and raised his eyebrows. "A headache?"

"Yes. You could just…hold me." Her lower lip trembled. "That would be nice."

He thought she'd said that for the benefit of the bug planted under the night table, but when he lay down, she rested her head on his shoulder. "I can't pretend," she whispered. "Not now."

Just as well. He'd have a tough time pretending, too.

When had things gotten so complicated? Hell, who was he kidding? Things had been complicated from the moment he took off after Jayne, chasing her in the darkness, determined to keep her safe at any cost.

No, not at any cost. The kid came first. Once he got

Drew out of here and safely into the hands of his grand-parents, then he could sort out this thing with Jayne.

Thing. Why did he have such a hard time calling this what it was? A relationship. Like it or not, he and Jayne had a *relationship*. It was convoluted, it had come out of nowhere, and there were moments when he was sure it was downright impossible. But he couldn't deny that it existed and was growing stronger.

He didn't have time for a relationship. Women came and went, but his job was his life. There was no room for a woman who would want his time, his attention, his commitment. Until the nightmares stopped, he didn't dare veer from the course he'd set for himself.

"Boone?" Jayne snuggled close. "What are we going to do? When we leave here, I mean."

Her voice was low. Maybe Marsh—or Gurza, if that was who was listening—could hear her words, and maybe not. It all depended on how sensitive that little bug was. "I don't know." He paused. "I do know I don't want things to end here."

Jayne snuggled against him. "Good." Was she being real? he wondered. Or was it Jayne the actress?

"Your father will hate me," he said.

Jayne laughed lightly. "No, he won't."

"Fathers always hate me. Especially fathers like yours." He shook his head.

"My father is a good man," Jayne said. "He loves me. And he'll adore you because I…adore you."

Boone's heart contracted. Well, at least now he knew she was playing for the hidden microphone. "I wish I could believe that."

Jayne seemed quite comfy, snuggled against him with her arm draped over his chest. "I feel safe here," she said, her voice much too low for any microphone to pick up.

Boone's voice was just as low when he answered, "You shouldn't."

Chapter 13

Jayne awoke from a sound sleep, her nose buried in Boone's bare chest, her arm draped over his side and one leg trapped between his. She didn't move for a moment; this was just too nice. Warm and comfortable and more right than she could have imagined.

She had always known, of course, that there were men out there who were made like Boone. He was big, hard and strong, with sculpted muscles and not an inch of fat on his body. Looking at him was definitely not a chore. She'd always assumed that men who looked like this fell into the category of "more muscles than brains," but she knew that wasn't true of Boone. He most definitely had a fine brain. And a heart.

Was she fascinated with him because he was so different from the other men she'd known? Life with her father kept her among lawyers, politicians and accountants. They were fine men, she supposed, but often they were also ambitious and calculating. Boone was honest in a way none of them had ever been.

A month ago she would have gotten out of this house the moment she'd discovered that something was wrong. Her father had always taught her to take care of herself, to put herself first. But Boone, who put his life on the line for her and for Drew and for countless other children, had made her see that it wasn't always right to run. He made her want to do something important, to be willing to risk her life for something she cared about. Or for someone.

Eventually she very gently moved away. Boone didn't get enough sleep. She didn't want to wake him while he slept so deeply.

Without making a sound, Jayne gathered clean clothes and headed for the bathroom. With the door closed, she ran a bath, sitting on the side of the tub and running her fingers through the water while the tub filled.

When they got out of here, would she ever see Boone again? The idea that she might not caused her heart to skip a beat. It made no sense that she slept better with him than without him, that he made her feel safe, that she loved his unfashionable long hair and his scowl and his hands and his leather jacket and…him. She cared for him deeply, in a way she had never cared for anyone else, and it made no sense.

He definitely wasn't what anyone would call her type, but there was more to Boone Sinclair than met the eye. Yes, he was big and occasionally crude, and sexy in a bad-boy kind of way. But there was more. He had a good heart and a deeply ingrained sense of justice. He cared about people, though getting him to admit it would probably be tough. There was tenderness in his kiss, the kind of tenderness that could not be manufactured for seduction. It was real. Honest. Heaven above, she loved the way he kissed.

Boone cursed less now than he had when she'd first met him. He did this for her, she imagined, even though he would never admit that he cared one whit what she thought of him or his language. He didn't want anyone to know what a sweet man he really was.

She'd given up on men after her disastrous engagement to Dustin. Until recently she hadn't realized that she'd given up so completely, but what else could you call a search for perfection? Boone wasn't perfect. No one was. But sometimes she thought that maybe, just maybe, he was perfect for her.

One fact she knew for sure: Boone didn't want her in order to get to her father; he didn't have any ulterior motives. He was positively repulsed by the world she came from. If he wanted her at all, it was for herself.

If he wanted her at all.

After her bath, Jayne dried off and dressed quickly, slipping on a blue cotton dress that would be perfect for the day. She brushed out her hair, dabbed on a little lipstick and stepped into plain white sandals.

From everything she'd heard, little boys rose with the sun. Maybe she could catch Drew and his nanny at breakfast, and once breakfast was over, she could ask Drew to show her his room. Kids always like to show off their rooms, right? And her interest in the little boy would be purely natural. Completely understandable.

Jayne left the room as quietly as she'd left the bed, without making a sound.

He fought the wind as the motorcycle sped down the winding road. He was home. He knew this was home because the trees and the kudzu he flew past reminded him of Alabama. This even smelled like home, clean and brisk and humid. For a moment, it was a good dream.

"You're going to blow it again," the voice behind him said.

Boone swerved. The motorcycle almost went off the road, but he was able to recover. Boone glanced over his shoulder, and sure enough, it was Patrick riding behind him. Red hair. Freckles. At least this time he didn't look dead.

"Hold on," Boone ordered.

"No," Patrick said defiantly. The kid refused to hang on to Boone as he should. He sat on the back of the bike's seat, unsteady. Wobbling and uncertain and cocky. Dammit, the boy was going to fall!

"You have really made a mess of things this time." Patrick shook his head slowly. "When are you ever going to learn?"

"Everything's fine," Boone insisted. He tried to pull the motorcycle to the side of the road, but the bike wouldn't cooperate. "I have everything under control."

Patrick laughed. "Do you really believe that?"

Boone tried to ignore the kid on the back of the bike and keep his eyes on the road, which was heading into a hairpin curve. The speed increased, the trees and the kudzu became a vast green blur, and the motorcycle left the road and took flight…

Boone rolled over and reached for Jayne—and found himself alone in the big bed. He cursed as he rolled upright, and then he remembered the damn bug that was planted under the bedside table. Did he talk in his sleep? God, he hoped not.

The nightmare was still with him, in unpleasant flashes of memory. Was that why he felt panicky? The dream? Or was his heart pounding a mile a minute because Jayne was gone?

"Jayne?" he called, standing and heading for the bathroom. The bathroom door was open. No Jayne.

He dressed quickly. Dammit, she knew better than to roam around this house on her own! Marsh was somehow connected to Gurza, and Gurza was a very bad man.

The house was big, but not *that* big. He walked toward the center wing of the house, where the living room, dining room, kitchen and library were located. There were a couple of other rooms that looked as if they were rarely used. He listened carefully and heard nothing. He hated the silence. Silence was not good.

Finally he heard something coming from far away. A child's laughter. He headed for the south wing, but then heard the laughter again. It didn't sound any closer, but even farther away.

Boone spun and headed back to the center of the house. This time he heard Jayne laugh, and he followed the sound unerringly.

He found them in the courtyard, Drew and Jayne sitting on the tile floor surrounded by toy cars and homemade ramps. For a moment he just watched, while his heart returned to a normal rhythm.

It wasn't fair that one woman should be so beautiful, he mused as he leaned against the doorjamb and watched. Jayne had a pretty face, her skin was fair and unblemished, her hair was that fascinating red-gold. But none of that made her beautiful. It was the glow of her smile, he decided. No. It was a glow from deep inside, and the warmth was always there. Smile or no smile, she…glowed.

He could just scoop them both up right now—Jayne

and the kid—and carry them out of here. The truck was out front and if he was fast enough… He scanned the area. The nanny sat at a table not far from Jayne and Drew. She wouldn't be any problem. But Harvey was inconspicuously seated not ten feet from Jayne, sipping a coffee and only every now and then lifting his eyes to check them out. Who was Harvey watching? Jayne or Drew? Didn't matter. Harvey was armed.

Boone had noticed, when the man carried his duffel bag in last night, that he held his left arm differently from his right. Sure sign of a shoulder holster. So much for Marsh's aversion to guns. Maybe he only had an aversion to weapons carried by anyone other than his employees.

Jayne finally realized he was there. She lifted her head and her smile changed. For him. Then she lifted a hand and crooked a finger, silently calling him over.

"We're playing demolition derby," she said as Boone approached.

Drew lifted his chubby face, those big brown eyes beautiful in their own heart-grabbing way. "Wanna play?"

Boone dropped to the floor and took the little metal car Drew handed him. "Why not?"

"As far as I can tell, the object of the game is to hit as many cars as possible," Jayne said.

"Yeah!" Drew said with a huge smile.

"I used to play this game with my brothers," Boone said, tapping his little car against Jayne's.

"I don't have any brothers," Drew said with a quick frown. "But sometimes Unca Corbin or Mr. Harvey play cars with me."

"That's nice," Jayne said sweetly.

Boone was instantly riled that the child actually played with an armed gunman, a thug like Harvey.

Drew leaned slightly toward Boone. "Miss Jayne plays like a girl," he confided in a whisper.

"I know," Boone whispered back.

They spent a few minutes banging their cars together, Drew laughing with delight at the simple game. When he tired of that, he began to run his favorite car over the ramps he'd fashioned from blocks and a couple of well-used children's books.

Boone leaned toward Jayne and whispered in her ear, "Don't you ever do that again."

"Do what?" she asked, wide-eyed.

"Get up and leave without telling me where you're going."

She smiled. "But you were sleeping so well. I didn't want to bother you."

Sleeping well? He was glad to know he hadn't given away the nightmare by tossing or talking in his sleep. Either that or she'd left before the nightmare had begun. Didn't matter. He wanted to know where she was at all times. He warned her with a glance.

"All right," she finally agreed reluctantly. "For goodness' sake, you're such a worrywart."

He leaned over and kissed her, telling himself that it would be the right thing to do for those who watched. It wasn't a deep kiss, just something sweet and touching to start the day with.

"Yuck!" Drew covered his eyes with both hands. "Kissing!"

Boone smiled as he pulled away from Jayne. "It's not so bad, kid. Just give yourself a few years."

They played for a while longer. The nanny stayed put and so did Harvey. How was he going to get Jayne and

Drew out of here without anyone getting hurt? Dean was waiting for a signal, and when the time came, Dean, Clint, Del and Shock would move in—with force if necessary.

He'd rather get Jayne and Drew out of here quietly if possible.

His first clue that Marsh was about to arrive on the scene came when the nanny stood up quickly. Harvey didn't stand, but his posture changed.

"Well, everyone's up early today," Marsh said as he stepped into the courtyard, smiling but not sounding pleased. "Lacey," he said to the nanny, "shouldn't Drew be working on his letters this morning?"

"Yes, sir," she said. "Come on, Drew. Playtime's over."

Jayne protested. "But we were having so much fun." She stood up when Drew did, and the little boy took her hand.

"Can Miss Jayne come see my room?"

Boone rose slowly to his feet.

"Perhaps after lunch," Marsh said tightly.

"Okay." Drew released Jayne's hand and turned his face up to her. "See you later, Miss Jayne." His eyes flitted to Boone. "You, too, Unca BooBoo."

Boone sighed and looked down at Jayne. "Why do I have the feeling this BooBoo thing is going to stick?"

She just smiled.

Marsh approached. He smiled, too, but something about his expression was tight. Uneasy. "You looked lovely sitting there playing with Drew. I imagine you'll be a wonderful mother someday."

A new bloom came to Jayne's cheeks. "I do love children," she said. "Maybe…someday."

"And what about you?" Marsh said, turning to Boone. "Do you love children, too?"

"Not particularly," he said.

Jayne slapped him playfully on the arm. "Boone!"

"Drew is a cute kid," he said defensively, "but for the most part, kids are a lot of trouble."

Jayne huffed. "*You're* a lot of trouble, but that doesn't mean you're not lovable." She blushed furiously.

Marsh turned to a waiting Benita and ordered coffee and sweet rolls to be brought to the courtyard. Jayne watched as Lacey and Drew disappeared into the house.

Boone glanced at Harvey. The big man didn't make a move to follow Drew and the young nanny. Damnation, Harvey wasn't guarding the kid; he was watching Jayne.

Jayne sensed that Corbin's hospitality was already wearing thin. They'd spent most of the morning talking politics. He was definitely interested, perhaps too interested, but the buoyancy she had seen in the Hollywood producer yesterday was gone. If not for Drew, she'd be on her way back to Flagstaff this afternoon.

Instead, she held Drew's hand as he led the way to his room. Lacey stayed directly behind them.

They'd had lunch; she and Boone, Corbin and Drew. And after the meal was over, Drew once again asked if he could show Miss Jayne his room. Corbin had consented. Boone had stood up as if he planned to join them, but Marsh kept him behind with questions about Alabama. Something about scouting for a location, or so Corbin said.

As they walked down a long wide hallway, Jayne wondered if Lacey would be a problem when it came time to get Drew out of here. The nanny was a quiet person who didn't smile much, but perhaps when she and Drew were alone, she was different. She hoped so. Drew needed a happy caretaker.

"This way," Drew said, picking up the pace and all but dragging Jayne through an open doorway.

She walked into a brightly decorated room filled with toys, a single school desk and a television complete with VCR. She'd seen day-care centers smaller and less well-equipped than this.

"This is my playroom," Drew said. "Miss Lacey is teaching me my letters, but we just play most of the time. Maybe next year I'll go to a real school."

"Maybe so," Jayne said softly.

Drew pulled her through another doorway into a plain but very nice bedroom, simply decorated in white and yellow. "This is Miss Lacey's room," Drew explained as he led Jayne to yet another doorway.

His own bedroom was decorated as the playroom was, in bright primary colors. It was the kind of room every child dreamed of having, except for the wrought-iron bars on the windows.

Jayne glanced around. "What a lovely room," she exclaimed. There were two doorways. One that led back to Lacey's bedroom and one that opened onto a bathroom. How on earth were they going to sneak Drew out of here?

Drew dropped her hand as he headed back to the playroom. Jayne lagged behind and walked beside Lacey. "This is very nice," she said. "Have you been here long?"

"Just a few months," Lacey said softly.

"Do you like working here?"

"Of course." Lacey sounded positive, but her eyes…her eyes were uncertain.

If there were listening devices in the guest rooms, there were surely microphones hidden throughout the house. Perhaps security in this wing was even tighter, since this is where Corbin and Drew spent most of their time. As Jayne walked into the playroom where Drew had already begun to construct a building out of brightly colored blocks, she looked around. The security camera in the corner was there for everyone to see.

Lacey definitely seemed nervous to have Jayne there observing. Maybe that was just the young woman's manner, but it didn't seem right to Jayne. Not right at all. If the nanny and the child were alone, would Lacey be on the floor building something out of blocks along with Drew?

"Drew seems to have every toy imaginable," Jayne observed.

"Mr. Marsh sees that his nephew gets anything he wants, as long as it's appropriate for his age."

Again it looked to her as if Drew was being more than well taken care of.

"This is such a nice place to work, but it's so far away from everything," Jayne observed casually. "Don't you miss…going shopping or to the movies?"

"Not really," Lacey said, her voice remaining low. "I owe Mr. Marsh so much, and if I want anything, he gets it for me."

"You owe him?" Jayne asked.

Lacey nodded. "I left home when I was seventeen. For a long time I was living on the streets. Mr. Marsh took me in, and I haven't had to…to struggle to survive since."

"How old are you now?"

"Nineteen."

"You should be in school," Jayne said.

"I'm happy here."

Jayne looked into Lacey's pale eyes and she didn't believe her. Not for a minute. "Are you and Corbin... involved?"

Lacey blanched. "No."

Jayne didn't believe that was a complete answer, but she didn't know the girl well enough to push. Not yet.

"Drew needs his nap," Lacey said, guiding Jayne to the door. "If he doesn't get one, he'll be cranky tonight."

"I understand," Jayne said as she stepped into the hallway.

Lacey closed the door practically in her face. Jayne took a deep breath. Now what? Out of the corner of her eye, she caught movement at the opposite end of the hallway. Harvey stood there, seeming very casual, checking out the inch or so of white cuff that peeked out of his jacket sleeve.

As Jayne headed back to the center of the house, she was quite sure Harvey followed. She didn't look back and he didn't make a sound, but she knew he was there. A chill danced down her spine.

She was going back to her room, hoping that maybe she'd find Boone there, when he stepped out of the library and took her arm.

"There you are, sugar," he said with a smile. "Did you miss me?"

"In the past fifteen minutes?"

"I missed you." He led her down the wide hallway and through the glass doors into the courtyard, then headed for the fountain that bubbled and sprayed. There he sat, dragging her down not to sit beside him, but onto his knees. He locked his arms around her and nuzzled her neck.

"I don't know if there's security out here or not," he said softly, "but if we keep our voices low and stay close to the fountain, we should be okay. What did you find?"

Jayne rotated so she faced Boone and laid her head on his shoulder. "Impossible. You have to go through an outer room, where there's at least one security camera, and then through Lacey's room just to get to Drew's. There are bars on the windows, too."

Boone cursed, low and very clearly.

"Is it possible that Corbin doesn't know that Drew was kidnapped? That maybe this Gurza told him a sad story and asked him to keep the boy here? Drew is well treated, and Corbin seems to adore him."

Boone shook his head. "Then why the lie about Drew being his nephew?"

"I don't know." She cupped Boone's cheeks and kissed him quickly. "I think we should take Lacey with us."

"The nanny?" His lips were close to hers.

"She's a runaway," Jayne said. "She says she's happy here, but I don't believe her."

"She might be just as big a part of this as Marsh is."

"If she's not, and if Corbin is as crooked as you seem to think he is, then he might take his anger out on her when we take Drew out of here."

Boone parted his lips, paused, then whispered, "Fudge."

Jayne kissed him again, soft and lingering. "Now what?"

"I'm not sure. We have a problem."

"What kind of problem?" There were so many!

"I came in here with three possible ways to signal Dean. My cell phone doesn't get a signal out here, and the fireworks I stored in the bottom of my duffel bag are gone, and so is the backup gun I'd stashed there. I suspect Harvey took them when he carried my bag in last night. He's watching us, by the way."

"What about the third signal?"

Boone sighed and tightened the arms that encircled her. "Last night I left my truck parked in the drive out front. I looked out the front window while you were with Drew and Lacey. It's gone."

"I only caught a glimpse of it through the open door, but it was rather...unsightly. Maybe Corbin had it moved." She rested her head on his shoulder. "The third signal is in the truck?"

"You could say that."

Boone's hand caressed her back. "You should've gotten out of here when you had the chance. Now...everything's complicated."

Jayne smiled and rubbed her nose against his. "Well, for once in my life being a senator's daughter might come in handy. Daddy knows where I am, and Corbin is well aware of that fact. They actually spoke on the phone. I'm safe here. He wouldn't dare try anything."

"Then you should go now. We stage a fight, you insist that Harvey drive you back to Flagstaff—"

"No." She briefly pressed her lips to Boone's. "I'm not leaving here without Drew or without you. Or without Lacey," she added. "Besides, if I leave the house, Corbin isn't likely to ask you to stay."

"So now you're out to save the world all by yourself?" Boone's lips brushed hers enticingly, but his voice was angry.

"Not by myself," she whispered. "And three people

are hardly the world.'' She skimmed her fingers across the back of his neck.

''Stop this,'' Boone whispered testily.

''I can't help it. I just can't walk out of here and leave three people—''

''Not that,'' he interrupted sharply. ''We're under constant surveillance, Marsh took my gun away, Harvey—who most definitely has a gun—is following you around like an ugly guard dog, I have no idea how we're going to get out of here…and right now I'm thinking with my favorite body part.''

''I know,'' she whispered with a wicked grin.

She put her mouth close to his ear. Long hair tickled her cheek. ''When we get out of here, you really should make a visit to Mississippi. Hooker Bend isn't all that far from Birmingham.''

''Hooker Bend?'' he repeated.

''Named for the founder,'' she said primly. ''Not an occupation.''

''If you say so.''

She ignored the shift in the conversation and continued with purpose. ''You could drive over for Sunday dinner. Meet Daddy and Mother and Grandmother. Maybe stay for a few days.''

''With Daddy?'' Boone asked suspiciously.

Jayne drew back so she could see his eyes. ''With me.''

Boone didn't answer, and the time for a response came and went. Corbin stepped into the courtyard.

''There you are,'' he said cordially. ''I feel guilty for leaving my guests to their own devices, though you two do seem more than capable of entertaining yourselves.''

Jayne kept her arms around Boone's neck and turned to smile at Corbin. He didn't look at all like a man who would become involved with criminals.

But then, Boone didn't look at all like an angel.

Chapter 14

Jayne had insisted on going back to her room to dress for dinner. Boone didn't understand why. Her blue dress was nice enough. She looked great. Besides, he didn't like having her out of his sight for any longer than necessary.

He wasn't changing for dinner. Besides, all he could do was trade one pair of jeans and one black T-shirt for another. Marsh hadn't excused himself to change, either. He wore another loose outfit, blue today, instead of beige. There was some kind of embroidery down the front. Boone found his clothing very strange, but then, it was probably some Hollywood thing.

He and Marsh had nothing in common and nothing much to talk about when Jayne was absent. Except, of course, Jayne. Even this afternoon, when Marsh had started asking Boone questions about possible shooting locations in Alabama, the conversation had quickly turned to the senator's lovely daughter.

Boone couldn't quite figure out Marsh's interest in her. It didn't seem personal. If that was the case, the producer hid his intentions well. He seemed almost amused by the idea of Jayne and Boone together. Never jealous, just a little bit too interested. More often than not, the conversation turned to Jayne's relationship with her father. Marsh was obviously out to build a relationship of his own with the senator.

It made a twisted kind of sense when Boone thought about it. Marsh was working with Gurza. He was doing his best to associate himself with a U.S. senator, create some financial and social ties. When it came time for a favor, the senator would be put in a very bad position. *Senator Barrington, would you like to help us out of this jam, or would you like it known that your last campaign was financed in part with drug money?*

When Jayne walked into the living room where Boone and an antsy Marsh waited, time seemed to stop.

No woman should be able to do this to him, Boone thought almost angrily. Jayne wore a calf-length sleeveless white dress, white heels and those pearls around her neck. She wore makeup she didn't need, but not too much of it. She was classy and artlessly seductive, and she too easily crawled beneath his skin.

He couldn't believe she'd actually invited him to Mississippi for Sunday dinner. Where he came from, an invitation to Sunday dinner was serious business. He wanted her; every now and then he actually thought he needed her. But Sunday dinner with the family? No way.

"I hope I didn't keep you waiting," she said with a smile.

Marsh rose to his feet. "Not at all. But I do believe dinner is ready. It's such a lovely evening that I asked

Benita to serve us in the courtyard.'' With a wave of his hand he indicated that it was time to go.

Boone reached Jayne before Marsh did and offered her his arm. ''You look good,'' he said softly.

''Thank you.'' She held on to his arm just a little bit too tightly as they walked toward the courtyard.

Jayne was scared. She would never admit it, and she wasn't scared enough to run, but she was definitely scared.

And still she stayed. That was real bravery, to his way of thinking. When a woman did what was right even though she was scared half out of her mind, that was courage. Jayne wasn't equipped for this kind of thing. She wasn't trained for undercover investigation. Almost unconsciously he gave her an encouraging comforting squeeze.

The courtyard had been suitably lit for the evening ahead. The illumination came from a couple of well-placed lamps, the moon, lights in the fountain and a few candles. When Jayne asked about Drew, Marsh informed her that his nephew had eaten earlier. This was an evening for the adults.

Music drifted from hidden speakers. The candles flickered. The fountain misted and gurgled, and a gentle breeze ruffled the leaves of hearty plants. The wine was good, the meal—served by Benita and her young assistant—was tasty, and through it all Boone saw nothing but Jayne.

And that was very dangerous for a man in his position. Being blinded by anything, especially a woman, could get him killed.

As if to prove his point, Harvey wandered into Boone's line of vision on the other side of a large window. How long had the man been watching? All the while, no doubt.

Dinner talk was politics and movies, a conversation Jayne and Marsh both participated in eagerly. Boone made the occasional comment, but for the most part he silently pondered the mess his life had become.

When the meal was finished and an awkward silence filled the air, Jayne turned her eyes to Boone and offered her hand. "Dance with me?"

He took her hand and stood, and she rose with him. "I'm not very good."

"I bet that's not true."

Fortunately the music that drifted from the speakers was slow, though it had a Latin beat that was anything but dull.

He took Jayne in his arms and they began to move. They knew each other well. There was no awkwardness in the way they moved, no hesitation. He led and she followed. Her body fit against his as if it had been made for him. Nothing in the world felt so good, smelled so fine. They remained silent as he gradually danced her toward the fountain, and Boone was glad of the silence. It gave him a moment to simply hold Jayne. He was afraid that holding Jayne was a pleasure he wouldn't be able to enjoy much longer. Yeah, he was definitely in over his head.

"Tonight?" she whispered in his ear as they danced by the fountain.

He nuzzled her neck and nibbled on her earlobe. "Just before dawn. I'm going to have to get to my truck. Otherwise we're on our own, and without a weapon we could be in serious trouble."

"What about Lacey?"

"If she wants to come along, she can. If not, we'll

have to leave her behind. I won't drag her out of here against her will.''

''Good enough.''

The music ended and they stopped dancing. Boone backed up a step and took Jayne's face in his hands, brushed his thumbs over her cheeks and lowered his head for a quick kiss. ''If we get out of here in one piece,'' he said as he slowly took his mouth from hers. ''I'm going to tan your hide.''

''Okay,'' she whispered.

''I mean it, Jayne.'' There was a warning in his voice as he put his mouth to her ear. ''If you get hurt, if things go wrong…''

''Boone,'' she whispered softly, ''look at me.''

He stared into her eyes. She wasn't as afraid now as she had been earlier. She was calm. Serene. And as he looked at her, she mouthed the words *I love you.*

Boone abruptly led her back to the table where an amused Marsh waited. ''Cigarettes,'' he said sharply. ''I left a pack in the glove compartment.'' Jayne sat, but Boone remained standing. ''I noticed that you had someone move my truck,'' he said to Corbin. ''Where is it?''

''In the garage,'' Corbin said. ''I'll have Harvey collect your cigarettes, but I will have to insist that you not smoke in the house.''

''I can get my own damn cigarettes,'' Boone snapped.

Jayne sighed. Obviously she shouldn't have been so open about what was on her mind. Apparently Boone didn't want her to love him. Well, too bad. She did and he needed her, whether he realized it or not.

Daddy would take some convincing, she supposed,

and Mother would be horrified at first. Grandmother would love Boone as she did, though. The woman had a knack of seeing right through people at first meeting.

Corbin had Harvey lead Boone to the garage, leaving the two of them alone.

"You two make an interesting couple," Corbin said as soon as Boone was gone.

"I suppose we do," Jayne admitted.

"Watching you dance, I could tell that you and Boone are…close."

"Oh," Jayne said. "Where are my manners? Would you like to dance?"

Corbin waved off her offer with a dismissive hand and a shake of his head. "No, thank you."

Just as well. Dancing with Boone had been wonderful. The same simple steps with Corbin Marsh would surely be awkward. There was a moment of strained silence, and then Corbin set his eyes on her in a calculating way.

"I could help you, you know."

"With what?"

Corbin smiled. "A haircut, a nice suit, a few lessons on decorum, and Boone could be whipped into shape so that the senator won't be…unpleasantly surprised when they meet. It wouldn't be any different from preparing a green actor for a new role. I assume Boone and your father will be meeting soon," he added.

"Yes, but…no," Jayne said. "Yes, they will be meeting soon, but I don't want Boone to change. I don't want him to cut his hair and dress differently and pretend to be someone he's not. I adore him just the way he is. Daddy will learn to love him."

Corbin's eyebrows lifted in mild surprise. "I doubt that very much."

"You don't know my father like I do." It was true. If Boone made her happy, her father would eventually accept him.

"I didn't mean to make an unwanted and unpleasant suggestion," Corbin said, reaching for his wine. "Let's change the subject, shall we?"

"Good idea."

Jayne's eyes flitted to the door. She didn't like having Boone so far away, not even for a few minutes. She felt safer when he was beside her. And more…real. How was she supposed to chitchat with Corbin as if nothing was going on? What choice did she have?

"Do you have a birthmark?" Marsh asked without warning.

The question caught Jayne by surprise. She blushed warmly, opened her mouth to answer, then closed it without saying a word. No matter how she tried, she couldn't come up with a proper way to tell Corbin Marsh that she had a birthmark on her rear end.

He lifted a hand, palm out. "Never mind. It's just that Drew has a small reddish mark on his side, and I had heard that sometimes they fade. I was simply curious."

"I do have a birthmark," Jayne finally confided. "And it has not faded one bit."

"Is it red?" Corbin asked, seemingly only casually interested.

"No, it's…" Jayne blushed again. "I'd really rather not talk about my birthmark if you don't mind."

Corbin leaned back in his chair and smiled like a man who knew something he should not.

Everything was set. As set as it was going to get, anyway. Boone had been taken to the truck, which was locked in a large separate garage, and then cursed for Harvey's benefit when he'd found no cigarettes in the glove compartment.

The lock on the garage door was electronic and would be tough to get past, but the latch on the back door to that same garage would be easy to work when the time came.

He couldn't sit still. His heart pounded. His fingers danced. Boone's anxiety had nothing to do with the plan to get Drew and Jayne—and maybe Lacey—out of here. It had everything to do with those three little words Jayne had mouthed in the courtyard.

He tried to tell himself that she'd been pretending. But the sad truth was, when she'd mouthed those words to him, her back had been to Marsh and Harvey. There had been no one else to see.

When they got out of here, the break was going to have to be quick and fast. She'd go back to her life, and he'd go back to his. He wanted to tell her so, but right now he couldn't. She sat up in bed, sweet as sugar in her white nightgown, and he paced the room restlessly. He couldn't say a damn thing, because someone was listening.

Control. He could not afford to lose control. Not now.

"Boone, honey," she said softly, "come to bed."

He glared at her and shook his head. No matter how much he wanted to, he couldn't touch her. Not anymore. It didn't matter that when he looked at her, he ached. That when he'd first met her, he'd thought she was cute, and somewhere along the way she'd become the most beautiful, the sexiest woman he'd ever seen. Jayne was confused, and if he wasn't careful, he'd be next.

He needed to tell her that what she was feeling wasn't

real. It was a combination of gratitude, lust and adrenaline. If he sometimes felt himself growing attached to her, it was for the same reasons. He would probably always remember her, think about her, but they didn't have anything lasting and—heaven forbid—permanent.

And all he could do was stand here and pace and scowl at her.

He couldn't take it anymore. He crossed the room, dropped down by the bedside table and yanked the bug from the underside. It was wireless and had been attached with some kind of lightweight adhesive.

He shook a finger at Jayne. "Lock the door behind me. I'll be right back."

Jayne scrambled from the bed to do as she was told. As he stormed down the hallway, he heard the lock in the doorknob turn and catch.

Boone glanced into the living room, the library and the dining room as he passed. No sign of their host. He didn't care if he had to go all the way to Marsh's bedroom to do this.

He headed into the south wing, hearing the distant sound of Marsh's voice—and another, equally familiar voice. Surprised, stunned even, he paused for a moment and then continued. The voices grew closer, until he reached a closed door off the wide hallway. Without hesitating he threw the door open.

Marsh was seated at a large oak desk, and his eyes widened with surprise as Boone leaned into his office, the microphone offered between two fingers. "There are some things that go on under your roof that are none of your business," Boone said sharply. He tossed the microphone across the room. It landed, as intended, directly in front of Marsh. "Are there any more of these in the bedroom?"

"No," Marsh said calmly.

"If I find another one…"

"You have my word," Marsh said, lifting the bug and examining it closely. "Just the one."

Boone turned his head and looked squarely at the other man in the room. "Darryl," he said with a smile. "How's your jaw?"

"You…" The fat man took two long angry strides toward Boone. Boone didn't budge.

"One moment, Darryl," Marsh said. A lifted hand and those gentle words stopped the angry man's progress.

Darryl had a nasty bruise on his jaw, and one wrist was bandaged. Marsh had stopped him for now, but the big guy was obviously pissed off.

And Darryl was not the forgiving sort.

"Come in, Boone," Marsh said cordially.

Darryl took a step back, and Boone entered the office and closed the door behind him. "I didn't mean to stumble on a business meeting," he said, making his way for Marsh's desk.

"You damn near broke my jaw," Darryl seethed.

"You moron," Boone said, spinning around to face the thug. The memory of Jayne's discarded blouse with the knife through it enraged him, but he couldn't say a word. He shouldn't have been there to see that not-so-subtle threat. "If I'd wanted to, I could have shot you while you were unconscious. I could have shot you, instead of kicking the gun out of your hand. I could have kicked your sorry ass so hard you'd be in the hospital right now eating through a tube."

"So, I should thank you?" Darryl shouted.

"Yeah."

"Now, gentlemen," Marsh said, his voice level and

easy, "let me handle this. Darryl, stay where you are. Boone, have a seat." He indicated the chair directly before his desk.

Boone sat, every nerve on edge, every muscle on alert.

"Should I call you Boone? Or Becker? Who are you, really? The private investigator or the drug dealer? I have evidence that you are both. It's most frustrating."

Everything came together in an instant, making sense at last. Each piece of the puzzle fell into place. Boone grinned. "Why can't I be both? Sinclair when it suits me, Becker when that identity works best."

"Interesting idea."

It took everything Boone had not to jump off the couch and rush the man. The wrong move could get him killed, and if he was out of the picture, what would happen to Jayne and Drew?

"You should know, Mr. Marsh," Boone said calmly. "Or should I call you Señor Gurza?"

Marsh smiled widely. "When did you figure it out?"

"I didn't." Boone admitted. "I took a guess and you just confirmed it. Not a bad gig. Rich guy in pajamas by day, cutthroat drug dealer by night."

"Oh, I don't need to call on Joaquin nightly." Marsh leaned back in his chair. "Only on occasion. The name itself is enough most of the time. Darryl and Harvey do all the dirty work. Gurza is simply a necessary evil I drag out on occasion to keep things rolling smoothly." His smile faded. "What brings you to Arizona?"

"You," Boone answered. "At least, in the beginning that was the case. I came here to hook up with the infamous Joaquin Gurza, but then this halfwit here tried to shoot a senator's daughter. I had to do something."

"You recognized her right away?"

"Of course I did," Boone said as if he was insulted. "You talk about a world of trouble coming down on you if one of your men were to murder someone like Jayne. You'd never get the feds out of your backyard."

Marsh cast a cutting glance at Darryl, as he contemplated the possible consequences of such an action. Eventually he turned his cold eyes back to Boone. "What do you want with Jayne Barrington? You can't tell me you actually see anything in her. She's not your type. I knew that all along. I know people, I understand their motivations."

Boone grinned. "Yeah, yeah, I get it. It's the Hollywood-producer thing. *I know people.*" His grin died as he leaned forward, gripping the armrests of the chair. "I want the same thing you do. You're looking to get in bed with the senator. I'm just taking a more direct route than you are."

"Can I kill him now?" Darryl asked.

"Of course not," Marsh said testily, his eyes remaining on Boone. "If I wanted him dead, he'd be dead by now. Mr. Sinclair, are you still interested in doing business with me?"

"Of course."

Marsh looked over Boone's shoulder. "Darryl, Mr. Sinclair is now your superior. You screwed up big time, and Boone is correct. If you had actually killed Jayne, there would have been hell to pay. As a matter of fact, I'd like you to thank Mr. Sinclair for not killing you when he had the chance."

"You want me to do *what?*"

"Thank Mr. Sinclair. Now."

"Thank you," the big man grumbled.

Boone turned his head and grinned up at Darryl. "You're most welcome."

Chapter 15

Jayne didn't stay in bed very long after Boone left the room. A few minutes at best. She simply could not stay still. Where on earth did he think he was going, anyway, with a nasty gleam in his eye and that little microphone grasped in his hand? Nothing but trouble could come of this.

She took her bathrobe from the closet, slipped it on and belted it, and crept to the door. She opened it noiselessly, then very cautiously stuck her head into the hallway. Harvey was usually close by. He had a tendency to turn up in the oddest places, but tonight the hallway was empty. The man had to rest sometime, she imagined, and he no doubt thought her asleep and under audio surveillance.

Jayne tiptoed barefoot down the long hallway. The house was quiet, the nighttime kind of quiet that made you whisper even though there was no one around to hear even if you shouted. She should be in bed asleep. Boone should be beside her. Where had he gone?

She reached the living room before she heard the muted voices. A word, a laugh, a snippet of conversation. Without a second thought, Jayne headed into the south wing and toward those voices. It wasn't long before she was close enough to identify one of those voices as Boone's. Relief rushed through her. He sounded fine. Not at all as if he was in trouble. A moment later she recognized Corbin Marsh's voice. Jayne wrinkled her nose. They sounded awfully…friendly.

With her back to the wall, Jayne crept closer. She could hear them well now. The door was only partially closed.

"How far do you plan to take this?" Corbin asked, amused and amicable. Funny, until now she'd gotten the feeling that Marsh didn't like Boone at all.

"As far as I can," Boone answered.

"Marriage?"

"Eventually. I figure if I rush things, Jayne will get spooked, so I plan to take it slow." He laughed. "I might even convince her that getting married is her idea."

Jayne's heart sank, and she very slowly lowered herself so she was almost sitting on the floor, her back to the wall, her heart hammering.

"The senator will balk," Corbin warned.

"I don't think so," Boone said confidently. "Jayne's a spoiled little rich girl. She's accustomed to getting anything and everything she wants, and right now she wants me."

One of them sighed, loud and long. Marsh, she imagined. "And then what? Besides the obvious blackmail potential of having a drug-dealing son-in-law, what can the senator do for you?''

''The same thing he can do for you,'' Boone answered, ''Connections. Respectability. Friends in high places.''

They both laughed.

''It was reckless of me to invite Jayne here so soon after her ordeal, but from what Darryl told me, I figured you'd be close behind her,'' Corbin said.

''This is all for my benefit?'' Boone asked.

''Not entirely,'' Corbin confessed. ''Separately, you and Jayne are interesting. Together, the possibilities are mind-boggling.''

Jayne didn't move. She didn't even breathe. Her mouth went dry. Her heart thundered. Her knees went weak.

''It's a good thing you recognized her right away,'' Corbin said in that new friendly tone of voice. ''If Darryl had killed her, we'd still be fighting off the feds.''

''Don't I know it.'' A chair creaked. ''Look, I need to get back to bed. Jayne's waiting. Do I have your word that there are no other bugs in that room?''

''In the closet,'' Corbin said. ''Wedged between the top shelf and the wall. It doesn't get great reception, but it makes a decent backup.''

Jayne stood and walked, quickly and silently, down the hallway and away from the room where Boone and Corbin were behaving like such good friends. She didn't know whether to be hurt or angry or frightened. Had they been working together all along? She was such an idiot.

As she hurried to her room, she kept listening for Boone, waiting for him to come up behind her, wondering what he would do if he caught her.

Once in her room, she locked the door and leaned against it. Now what? She wasn't like Boone. She couldn't look at him and pretend she hadn't heard. But if he found out she knew what he was up to…

Jayne hung up her robe in the closet, then stretched to see if she could spot the listening device Corbin had told Boone was planted there. She couldn't. It didn't matter. She wasn't going to say anything. She wasn't going to make a sound for anyone to hear.

She crawled into the bed and pulled the covers to her chin, wishing she could just pull them over her head and hide. Unfortunately she didn't have time to hide. What about Drew? Had the boy really been kidnapped, or was that just another lie?

She didn't know what to believe. Too much had happened in the past few days. Did she really know Boone at all? She'd thought so, but now she wasn't so sure. He was definitely lying to someone, and he'd said it himself: lying was what he did best.

Maybe she should just play along until she got out of here. Then she could tell him that he was right; she didn't love him. She'd been caught up in the moment, nothing more. He'd have no choice but to give up his plan to use her. Convince her it was her idea to get married! The ego!

But she wasn't very good at pretending. She said what she thought, wore her heart on her sleeve. So far she'd been able to fool Corbin Marsh, but it hadn't been easy. She was not a good liar, not at all. Not like Boone.

The doorknob turned and the gentle rattling noise was followed by a soft knock. "Jayne?" Boone whispered. "It's me."

She said nothing. Maybe he'd think she'd fallen asleep and retreat to the bedroom across the hall. She certainly couldn't face him, not now. Tonight she'd actually told Boone that she loved him, and then…then she'd found out he wasn't like the rest. He was much worse.

The doorknob rattled some more, the lock gave way with a soft click, and Boone walked in. By the time the door swung open, Jayne had her back to him and her eyes closed.

She was asleep. Just as well. Morning was going to come early. Boone took the same tool he'd used to pop the lock and headed for the closet. He shifted the top shelf until he saw the bug, worked it loose and returned to the door. Using his best pitching arm, he threw the tiny microphone down the long hallway and then gently closed the door and locked it.

Remembering how easily he'd slipped past the lock, he grabbed a chair from the desk and propped it under the doorknob. He didn't trust anyone in this house but Jayne and Drew. And Drew was iffy. The kid liked his uncle Corbin too much.

Boone stripped to his boxers and lay on the bed, on *top* of the covers. He really should get a couple of hours of sleep himself, but he didn't think he would. Marsh and Gurza, one and the same. He never would have believed it. Del and Shock were going to have a field day with this one.

It took him a couple of minutes, but he finally realized that Jayne was not asleep. She was wound so tightly he could practically feel the tension radiating off her. Her breathing was erratic and uneven.

He rolled over, getting close so he could whisper in her ear. Marsh had said there were only the two bugs in this room, but he didn't trust the man as far as he could throw his hippie ass.

"What's wrong?"

"Nothing," she said tightly.

He put his hand on her hip. "Worried about tomorrow morning?"

"Yes."

He crawled under the covers with her. Hell, why not? This would be the last night he'd get to lie beside her. When he tried to draw her body against his—in a purely asexual manner of course—she froze.

"Relax," he whispered.

"I can't."

He wondered if he should tell her about Marsh, then decided against it. If she was this anxious already, she didn't need anything else on her mind.

It hit him, in an unpleasant way, that what was bothering Jayne probably had nothing to do with their plans for the early-morning hours. She'd told him she loved him, and he hadn't responded as she'd thought he would. No wonder she'd locked the door on him.

She was mad at him. Just as well. It would make the final break easier, he imagined.

"Maybe you should just sleep in your own room," she whispered.

"No way." Leave her unprotected? Try to rest when he couldn't see and feel her? It would never work.

She turned slowly and in a surprise move pulled the covers over her head and his. The bathroom light had been left on, but very little penetrated the coverlet and sheet. He couldn't see her face. "You were right all along," she said tightly. "This will never work. I don't know what I was thinking."

He touched her cheek. Was it damp? Or was that his

imagination? "It's been a wild week," he said softly. "We both went a little crazy. Don't worry about it."

"Once we get out of here, it's probably best that we don't see each other again."

"Yeah," he agreed. "That would be the way to go."

She sighed. "My father will be happy to pay you for your services."

He couldn't help but smile. "Oh, really," he said suggestively.

"Not *those* services, you…you Neanderthal."

He was going to miss her, dammit. And he didn't miss anyone. Not ever. Since this was their last night, he pulled her close. She didn't want to be held, her body language told him, but he didn't let go. Not yet. "I don't want your daddy's money. I don't want you to think this is…anything it's not." He didn't dare use the L-word. "But I'm glad I got to know you. You really are amazing."

"So are you," she muttered, and it didn't sound at all like a compliment.

When Jayne rolled over, presenting her back to him again, he let her go. Women. He'd never understand them. Maybe that was just as well.

Jayne didn't sleep much, but she did manage to doze. She was in no physical danger of course, not as long as Boone thought he still might cajole and seduce her into asking him to marry her. Last night she probably should have pretended to be infatuated with him, still. But she knew her limitations. Pretending not to know that Drew had been kidnapped was one thing. Looking Boone in the eye and pretending nothing had changed would be impossible.

A nudge from Mr. Wonderful woke her. It was still dark outside, but morning was coming.

"Let's go," he said.

The plan was simple. She'd go to Drew's room and fetch him, while Boone did something with the truck. How that was supposed to alert the others it was time to move in, she didn't know. For all she knew, no one was coming to help. She didn't know what to believe anymore.

She did know that as long as Boone had plans for her, she was safe, and if Drew had indeed been kidnapped, then perhaps he would be safe with her.

Unlike Boone, Jayne didn't have the clothes for skulking around in the predawn hours. She did have a pair of black slacks in her suitcase, and flat black shoes, but the yellow blouse she'd packed to wear with those trousers had been roundly dismissed by Boone. He tossed her one of his black T-shirts as she got dressed, and without comment she pulled the oversize shirt on. She also put on her pearls, which made Boone laugh.

"I'm not leaving them behind," she said, in answer to his derisive snort. "And I don't think carrying a purse over my shoulder is going to help matters any." He'd told her they'd leave with nothing but the clothes on their backs. And Drew of course. And Lacey, if she wanted to come with them.

He took her hand as they stepped into the hallway. She shook him off. His only response was a quick puzzled glance.

When they reached the center of the house, they parted company. Jayne headed for the south wing, where she'd collect Drew and Lacey, and Boone went through the kitchen to exit by that door and make his way to the garage.

The playroom was dark, but Jayne's eyes had adjusted, and she made her way through without a hitch. When she stepped into Lacey's room, she found the young girl sound asleep. Was it possible that Lacey really was happy here? That if she was awakened, she'd set off an alarm? Jayne knelt beside the bed and shook Lacey's shoulder. The girl immediately awoke.

"I'm taking Drew and getting out of here," Jayne whispered. "Would you like to come with us?"

Lacey hesitated only a moment before she nodded her head and sat up.

While Lacey dressed, Jayne crept into Drew's room. The child slept peacefully. Was this a mistake? Had he been kidnapped and used to bring an end to his mother's murder investigation? Or was he truly Marsh's nephew? Boone might very well be making her a kidnapper. He might be planning to use the child against Marsh.

It didn't matter. Boone and Marsh were both criminals. She wanted this child out of here and safe, whether it was with loving grandparents or...with her. He wasn't safe in this house. She knew that much, and she didn't need to know anything else.

"Drew," she called softly as she shook his shoulder. "Come on, honey."

His eyes blinked open. "It's still dark," he said sleepily.

"We're going to play a game," Jayne whispered.

"Turn on the lights," Drew said as he sat up, rubbing his eyes and yawning.

"I can't. This is a game we play in the dark." She offered her arms and Drew, still sleepy, came to her. "Be very quiet."

She carried a sleepy Drew, who rested his head on

her shoulder, into Lacey's room. The girl was already dressed in jeans and a navy-blue sweatshirt.

The three of them crept into the playroom, staying against the wall and out of range of the security camera. Boone was to meet them here as soon as he did his thing with the truck. Maybe there were more fireworks hidden in the jalopy, or some kind of transmitter was just waiting to be activated. Maybe there was nothing at all in the truck, and this was simply another lie.

"I'm too sleepy to play, Miss Jayne," Drew said softly.

"Shh. Why don't you go back to sleep, then?" she urged. She repositioned Drew in her arms. He was heavy, but not too heavy. He was also warm and trusting, as naive as she had once been. He quickly fell asleep and went limp against her.

"This isn't a good idea," Lacey said. The girl fidgeted nervously. "If Mr. Marsh catches us, he'll...he'll..."

"What?" Jayne whispered.

"He'll kill us all."

The lights came on, momentarily blinding Jayne. "Well, now, that's a little overly dramatic, don't you think?" Corbin asked.

He held a gun in his hand, and it was pointed at Lacey. Jayne stepped in front of the girl. "I couldn't sleep," she said. "I thought I'd see if Lacey and Drew wanted to take a walk with me. The red rocks just to the west of the house are so beautiful, and I haven't seen them at this time of day. I imagine—"

"Save it, Miss Barrington," Marsh said tightly. "I would dearly love to believe you. My life would be much less complicated if I could." His pale stare cut right through her. His lips went thin and hard. "But I don't. What a mess. I guess all three of you are going to have to go.''

A sleeping Drew snuggled his face against Jayne's shoulder, blocking out the light. Oh, she wanted him to sleep through this. The sight of his beloved uncle with a gun in his hand would surely be traumatizing.

''I was going to bring him back,'' Lacey whimpered. ''I was just playing along so I could—''

''Shut up,'' Marsh snapped. ''I took you in, cleaned you up, I even loved you, for a while.'' His mouth thinned. ''When I got tired of you, I gave you a job to keep you off the streets. And this is how you thank me. You and Drew will both pay for that mistake.''

''You wouldn't dare hurt this child,'' Jayne said. ''You love him, at least a little. And he adores you.''

Marsh's facial features went stony, and he finally looked his age. ''You're right,'' he said. ''I could never hurt Drew.'' He glanced into the hallway behind him. ''Fortunately my friend Darryl has no such reservations.''

Jayne gasped. She wasn't afraid of Boone, no matter what plans he had for her, and she wasn't afraid of Corbin Marsh. But Darryl terrified her; he always had.

The fat man stepped into view, taking a solid stance behind Marsh, a crooked smile blooming on his ugly face.

''I've been looking forward to seeing you again, *sugar*,'' Darryl said.

Jayne tightened her hold on Drew.

''Where's your boyfriend?'' Marsh asked, ignoring Darryl's threat.

''You tell me!'' Jayne snapped. ''After all, he's…he's just like you! He's a drug dealer and a liar and he doesn't care about anyone but himself.''

"You found him out, I see." Marsh shook his head. "Too bad."

"I don't care what you three do, I really don't." Jayne lifted her chin haughtily. "But Drew deserves better than to be raised in a house that's rife with criminals and…and thugs like Darryl."

"Rife?" Darryl repeated softly.

Marsh silenced his goon with a raised hand. "So you found out Boone was not who he claimed to be, and you decided to run. But you also decided to take my nephew with you. To…save him."

"Yes," Jayne whispered.

"Very noble of you."

It hit Jayne, with a dreaded finality that sat in her stomach like a boulder, that Boone wasn't coming. There was no signal. There was no planned rescue. She was on her own.

"He's a sweet innocent little boy," she said. "He doesn't belong here. Can't we make a deal? You let us go, and I swear not to tell anyone that things here are not what they seem."

Marsh shook his head. "I wish it was that sim—"

An explosion shook the house. Drew woke, Jayne cowered and Lacey squealed.

Corbin waved his gun at Darryl. "Go see what that was."

Darryl disappeared down the hallway, running, his heavy footfall fading rapidly, and Corbin Marsh stepped into the playroom as Drew rubbed a fist against sleepy eyes. "In the back of my mind I always knew I shouldn't mess with politics."

Chapter 16

Boone ran toward the house with the explosion reverberating behind him. Dean had concealed the explosive device in the passenger-seat cushions as a last resort. If Boone couldn't get to his cell phone or set off the fireworks, the truck could be rigged to blow.

It had taken longer than he had planned to get the timer on the device set. There had been a couple of annoying safety precautions to get past. Dean was nothing if not safety conscious.

Before he reached the kitchen door, Darryl burst from the house, gun drawn. Boone came to an abrupt stop. "Something in the garage blew up," he said. "Sabotage, I think."

Darryl looked toward the flames and then back at Boone. "How come you're running away from the explosion?" The grip on his pistol changed slightly. "Shouldn't you be checking it out?"

"I started to do just that, and then I got to worrying that there might be a second explosion coming."

"Oh." Darryl, not certain if he wanted to be convinced or not, stared at the flames erupting from the truck Boone had pulled out of the garage. His mind worked slowly, and within seconds the grip on his pistol changed. No, he wasn't buying it, but he couldn't be certain that Boone was lying, either.

Boone took the opportunity to kick the weapon out of Darryl's hand. The pistol went flying, Darryl howled, and Boone dropped down and rolled toward the pistol.

An enraged Darryl came around, meaty fist swinging. Boone avoided the fist and got in a good one of his own, a hefty blow to the stomach. Fighting Darryl was like wrestling a bear. Up close, there was no chance he could win.

He slipped out of Darryl's grasp and ducked when the man came after him like an enraged bull. When Darryl turned around, he got a boot in the face. The blow knocked him to the ground, but this time it didn't knock him out.

But he was stunned. Before Darryl had a chance to recover and come at Boone, he found himself facedown on the ground, the barrel of his own gun pressed against his neck.

"You're too late," the pinned man said with a hint of glee in his gruff voice. "Sinclair or Becker or whoever you are, Gurza's got your woman. There's no saving her this time."

Boone stuck the pistol in his waistband and snagged a roll of duct tape from an inside pocket of his jacket. In a matter of moments Darryl was bound and gagged and leaning against the back of the house, partially concealed by a thorny bush. Every time the big man moved, fighting his bonds, the prickly plant got him.

He didn't doubt for a minute that Darryl had been telling the truth. Marsh—Gurza—had Jayne. That meant he had the boy, too, and the nanny. Dean, Clint, Del and Shock would be here in a matter of minutes. Would they arrive soon enough?

Boone's heart hammered as he ran through the house, not bothering to be silent. He drew the weapon he'd taken from Darryl, ready to use it if he had to. Ready to do anything and everything.

A single light burned in the south wing. From Jayne's description of the rooms off the hallway, that was Drew's playroom. Boone raced toward it.

Jayne stood at the back of the room, a pajama-clad Drew in her arms. Lacey stood mostly behind Jayne, peeking around at Marsh, who had his back to the door. Three innocent pairs of eyes landed on Boone. Only Drew smiled.

"Unca BooBoo," he said.

Jayne cupped Drew's head and pulled it to her shoulder, urging him to go back to sleep, shielding him from the horrors of the night.

Marsh didn't bother to turn around. "We have a problem."

"So I see," Boone said as he stepped into the room. Jayne's accusing eyes landed on him.

"Her father knows she's here, but I can't very well let her go." Finally Marsh turned his head and looked at Boone. "What do we do with her?"

"We keep her here," Boone said, his voice steady. "She and I get married, we keep her close—"

"In your dreams," she snapped.

He warned her with his eyes, but she didn't seem to

understand what he was trying to tell her. "The way I see it, sugar, you have two choices. We get married. You keep your mouth shut and tell Daddy what I tell you to and nothing more, and everyone gets to live. You decline our generous offer…" He shrugged his shoulders. "Well, it would really be a shame to waste someone as pretty as you, but if we have no choice, we have no choice."

As Boone talked, he moved closer to Marsh. The man's gun was still pointed at Jayne. Until that changed, there wasn't much he could do. He'd never been one for talking his way out of a situation. His first instinct was to fight his way out. Right now his first instinct might very well get Jayne, as well as Drew and Lacey, killed.

Jayne's eyes filled with tears. Her chin trembled. She wasn't a bad actress, but she wasn't this good. Damnation, he thought, she believed what she was hearing. After everything they'd been through, she really believed that he and Marsh were in this together. Was that why she'd turned cold on him last night?

She must have left her room against his orders, overheard them talking and come to the wrong conclusion. Remembering what had been said in Marsh's office last night, he could only imagine what Jayne was thinking right now. She should have asked him last night, instead of keeping it all inside. Instead of believing the worst.

Why did he expect better of Jayne? Why did knowing she thought he was one of the bad guys hurt?

Right now none of that mattered.

"Make the right choice, sugar," he said. *Buy me a few more minutes.*

He heard Harvey, his step heavy as always, running down the hallway. "We got trouble!" the man shouted.

"News flash," Marsh muttered.

A breathless Harvey stopped in the playroom doorway. "Vehicles coming this way. Four of them, one from each direction. No telling how many men are in each vehicle."

Harvey looked at Boone suspiciously, his gaze dropping to the weapon Boone held.

"Where's Darryl?" Harvey asked.

"I have no idea," Boone answered coolly.

Harvey's gaze dropped to the weapon again. "Then why do you have his new pistol?"

Marsh spun, his weapon raised, and impulsively and angrily fired. Boone ducked, and Marsh's bullet hit the man standing in the doorway.

Before he could fire again, Boone grabbed Marsh's wrist and pushed the weapon aside, then turned his eyes to Jayne. Her heart stopped.

"Run," he ordered. "The courtyard."

Jayne didn't question Boone but held on to Drew with all her might and did exactly as he instructed. She ran. Lacey stayed close behind her, and a confused Drew, who had managed to fall asleep again before the shot was fired, held on tight. They had to step over a downed Harvey to get out of the room. Jayne was half-afraid that one of those meaty hands would shoot up and grab her by the ankle. But the man remained still.

A gunshot fired behind them and she flinched. But she didn't go back. First priority was getting Drew to safety. Boone could take care of himself, of that she was certain. Should she go to the courtyard as he'd instructed? Or run out the front door and hope for the best?

The look in his eyes when he'd told her to run made
the decision easy. She made a beeline for the courtyard.

Things were happening fast. She heard shouts from
inside the house. Breaking glass. Another gunshot. The
three of them burst into the courtyard.

"Look." Lacey pointed.

A man was scaling the wrought-iron fence. He never
paused, never seemed to think twice. He reached the
top and vaulted over, every move smooth and strong,
and landed easily on his cowboy-booted feet.

"Let's go," he said, heading straight for Jayne.

"Who are you?" she asked, holding Drew closer and
unable to trust anyone at this moment.

He gave her a quick grin. "Clint Sinclair."

"I should have known," she muttered. He was leaner
than Boone or Dean, and his hair was a shade lighter,
but the resemblance was strong.

"Let's go," he said again.

Jayne looked toward the house. "No," she whispered, thrusting Drew at Clint so he was forced to take
the child into his own arms. "I'm going back for
Boone."

A quick hand on her wrist stopped her. "Oh, no,"
Clint said softly. He no longer smiled. "I'm to get you
and the kid—" he glanced at Lacey "—and her, I imagine, out of here."

She'd doubted Boone. She'd given him the cold
shoulder when he'd needed her to be there for him.
When it was most important, she'd lost faith. She
wasn't going to leave him here, not like this. "More
than anything, Boone wants this child out of here."

"I know that." Clint did not release her wrist.

"That's your job, to get him out, to keep him safe."

"Yep."

"I don't know what I was thinking," she said, pretending to give up. "Boone can take care of himself."

Clint winked at her. "That he can."

The second Clint released her, she ran. "Get Drew out of here!" she called over her shoulder, reentering the house and turning toward the south wing.

The house was in chaos. Four men she had not seen during her stay here tried to find a route of escape. She knew they weren't with the small rescue party, since Boone had told her to look for Dean and those two DEA agents she'd met in Flagstaff. These men ran. They even broke windows and furniture in their panic to get out. Two other men she recognized as Agents Wilder and Shockley caught them and herded them together smoothly.

Dean was speaking to Benita and the young blonde who helped her in the kitchen. The two women were huddled together, offering no resistance as they answered Dean's heated questions about the number and locations of people in the house. Smoke from gunfire made the air hazy.

When Jayne entered the south-wing hallway, she saw Boone. He was on his knees, sort of. One knee was on the floor, the other pressed against a prone Corbin Marsh's back.

Boone raised his head as she neared. "What the hell are you doing here?"

Her throat was dry, her insides roiling. "I couldn't just...leave you."

"Yeah, you could." He reached into his jacket pocket and withdrew a roll of duct tape. "Get moving, sugar."

Something behind Boone moved. A wounded Harvey

came to his feet, slowly, silently. He reached into his jacket and drew a small gun from his shoulder holster.

"Behind you," Jayne whispered.

Boone drew his weapon, whirled and fired. Harvey fell, hitting the floor hard. While Boone was turned away Marsh scrambled to his feet and ran straight for Jayne, his pale eyes on her face. She saw the hate in them, felt it. He didn't have a weapon in his hands, but that didn't make her feel much better at the moment.

Boone took aim but didn't fire, and she knew why. She was in the way. A noise behind her caught Marsh's attention, and he cut away, running into the closest bedroom.

Dean ran from one end of the hallway, Boone from the other. But while Dean stepped immediately into the bedroom Marsh had disappeared into, Boone stopped before Jayne. He stared at her for a moment, then kissed her hard. "Get out of here," he ordered as he followed his brother.

She didn't want to leave, but she did. The only way she knew to show Boone that she trusted him was to do as he asked. Without question.

Clint's sole job, apparently, was to transport the innocent bystanders out of here. From inside the courtyard, he'd opened the wrought-iron gate with the same ease Boone had picked the lock on the bedroom door last night. He had a four-wheel-drive vehicle waiting, and Drew and Lacey were settled in the back seat and ready to go.

Jayne ran toward Clint. He waited, more patiently than most men would have, but still with the telling restless tapping toe of one cowboy boot.

"Are you trying to get me in trouble, Miss Barrington?" he asked as she climbed into the passenger seat.

She didn't bother to answer, but looked back at the house as Clint pulled away, his foot to the floor. The big pink house grew small very quickly.

Drew leaned over the seat and stared at Clint. "Are you a cowboy? You look like a cowboy."

"Nope," Clint said with a grin. "I'm not a cowboy. I'm a bullfighter."

"A bullfighter!" Drew repeated.

"Fancy name for a rodeo clown," Lacey said softly. "Anybody who's ever seen a bullriding competition knows that."

"You're a clown, too?" Drew asked. "Where's your red nose?"

"In my suitcase," Clint said without slowing down or turning his head. "Along with my big floppy shoes."

Drew giggled. "You don't look like a clown."

Jayne turned and smiled at Drew. "Honey, this clown is Uncle BooBoo's brother."

"He is?"

Clint shot her an amused glance. "Uncle BooBoo?"

"You can call him Uncle Clint."

Uncle Clint let out a hoot of laughter. "Uncle BooBoo. That's a good one."

Jayne looked back, but there was nothing to see. Already they were too far away. Boone would be all right. He was good, he was right...and he wasn't alone. Not this time.

Drew stared out at the landscape that sped past. "Miss Jayne, where's Unca Corbin?"

Jayne's heart sank. Corbin Marsh was a very bad man, but he'd been good to Drew. The little boy wouldn't understand what was happening. He'd already seen too much tonight. He'd seen things she hoped he forgot, maybe dismissed as a bad dream. She didn't know what to say.

Clint did. "Your uncle Corbin, he wanted you to have a really nice place to stay, since he can't take care of you right now. So he called your grandparents and asked them to meet you at the hotel where Miss Jayne is staying."

"He did?"

"Yep. They're really nice people. I talked to them myself on the telephone."

"Before she went away, my mama showed me pictures of my grandparents," Drew said in a small voice. "She said they were really nice and that my grandma makes the best chocolate-chip cookies in the world. She said that one day we would go live with them."

"They can't wait to see you," Clint said. "And I'll bet if you ask your grandma just right, you'll have chocolate-chip cookies every day for a year."

Boone kicked, he cursed, he threw the closest object—a crystal for God's sake—across the room. Corbin Marsh, aka Joaquin Gurza, had disappeared.

"I had him!" he raged. "I had my knee on his spine and the duct tape in my hand."

"What happened, man?" Shock asked.

"Jayne showed up out of nowhere, Harvey tried to put a bullet in my back, everything went wrong."

"Bad luck," Shock grumbled.

Harvey was dead, Darryl was in custody, and several other servants were being questioned. Some of them were probably legitimate, but there was no telling how many of them were involved in Marsh's crooked business. After all, Harvey had done double duty as driver on occasion.

Clint had gotten away with Jayne and Drew and Lacey. Right now, not much else mattered. It was a comfort, knowing they'd escaped, knowing they were safe. Getting Drew out of Gurza's hands was another job successfully completed, another kid heading back where he belonged.

Knowing Jayne was safe touched him more deeply than a job well-done. He could breathe easier now. His heart didn't threaten to jump through his chest, as it had when he'd seen a gun pointed at her.

Nothing else mattered except that the two of them were safe. He sure would like to get his hands on Marsh, though.

Del found an escape hatch in the closet, a well-disguised door in the closet floor that opened onto a tunnel. Marsh was well and truly gone. Boone let loose with a few more curses.

Dean came up beside him, his head cocked to one side, one eye narrowed. "What did you say?"

"Huh?"

"I could've sworn you said...fudge."

Chapter 17

This had surely been the longest day of her life. Jayne fell onto the bed in her suite and let herself go boneless. Drew was safe with his grandparents. She'd never seen two people more relieved to see a child. The Pattersons were spending the night in this very hotel and would fly back to Atlanta in the morning. For now, Lacey was staying with them. They thought it might make the transition easier for Drew. Besides, Lacey didn't have a good home to go back to.

The luggage Jayne had left behind at Marsh's had been delivered by a young policeman carrying out orders from higher up. She'd been hoping Boone would make that delivery. Silly hope, she imagined, but still…

Since fighting off the reporters and shutting herself in her room, instructing the desk to screen her calls and talking to her father—who would be here in the morning—Jayne had enjoyed a hot bath and a good meal.

Security had finally run the last of the reporters off her floor.

So why couldn't she sleep?

Because Boone wasn't here. Because she knew that he realized she'd believed the worst of him. Why did she have such a hard time trusting her heart? She should have known that if Boone lied to anyone, it was Marsh. Not her. Never her.

She didn't want to be the kind of person who always expected the worst of those around her, who never loved completely enough to trust without question. Most of all, she didn't want Boone to leave before she had the chance to tell him she was sorry.

A knock on the door had her bounding off the bed. If that was another reporter, she was going to take someone's head off! She'd always gone out of her way to be friendly and cooperative with the media, but tonight she had asked—several times—to be left alone. You'd think they could give her one night of peace.

She belted her robe with an angry yank as she stalked to the door on bare feet and stood on tiptoe to peer through the peephole.

Jayne threw the door open and stared at Boone, who stood in the hallway looking worn-out and uncertain. He shifted from one foot to the other. "Dean told me you were in the same room as before. I just wanted to see for myself you're okay," he said.

Their eyes met. Jayne's insides tumbled and twisted. If she played it cool and calmly told Boone that she was just fine, thank you, he'd walk away and that would be the end. She didn't want him to walk away, and she could tell by looking at him that he didn't want to go.

Jayne reached into the hallway, grabbed Boone by the leather jacket and pulled him into the room. "Where

have you been? I was worried sick.'' She wound her
arms around his neck and held on. Oh, she loved the
feel of him. She'd been so worried she'd never hold
him again. ''I thought you weren't coming.''

He kicked the door shut and, his eyes still on her,
blindly bolted it behind him. ''I had to talk to the cops,
local and federal, and they came at me with a million
questions.'' He lifted Jayne off her feet and she wrapped
her legs around him. ''The whole time, I just wanted to
be here,'' he said, his nose rubbing hers, his mouth rak-
ing across her parted lips.

Jayne speared the fingers of one hand through his
hair. She couldn't hold him tightly enough. Every nerve
in her body was awake and aware, and her heart
pounded hard. She kissed him and he met her kiss hun-
grily. It was a kiss that said they had survived and they
were together and nothing else mattered. She wanted to
laugh and cry at the same time, but instead, she kept
kissing Boone. Long deep kisses. Short breathless ones.
Sweet kisses. Tongues dancing, barely touching and
then searching deeply.

Their mouths still fused, Boone carried her to the
bedroom. Jayne tasted so much in Boone's kiss and in
the desperate way he held her. He needed her, and he
still didn't understand why.

She didn't understand the why of it, either, but she
had passed that point. She didn't care why she loved
and needed and wanted Boone. What she felt was real
and right, and that was all that mattered.

Draped around him as they moved slowly toward the
king-size bed, she kissed Boone with everything she
had. His hands were big and firm and steady as he held
her close, his heartbeat against hers.

She couldn't get close enough; they couldn't kiss

deeply enough. Ribbons of promise wafted through her, a tingle here and a tremor there. As he lowered her gently to the bed and hovered above her, she just wanted him to love her.

She had never before been so completely over-whelmed by sensation. The scent of Boone, the press of his body against hers, the taste of his mouth and the sight of him hovering above her. And the sound of their shared breaths and Boone's whispering her name against her mouth.

''Jayne.''

She pushed his jacket off his shoulders and down, her hands skimming over his muscular arms. Her body pulsed and reached for his in so many ways. Her mouth, her hips, her fingers.

While she ran her hands beneath his T-shirt, soaking up his heat and his need, Boone untied the belt of her robe and whipped it away. The robe fell open, and he lifted the hem of her nightgown, snagged the edge of her panties with one finger and whisked them down.

He touched her intimately, and she responded more intensely than she had imagined she could. Her body throbbed and shimmied from head to toe, and so did Boone's. She felt it, his need for her, the way he spi-raled out of control just as she did.

''Now,'' she whispered, unfastening his jeans and lowering the zipper. Shoving the jeans and boxers down to free him.

He guided himself to her and then plunged deep and hard, filling her completely.

Jayne gasped, lifted her hips and rocked against him. And shattered with such force that she cried out loud. Boone climaxed, too, as her inner muscles clenched and quivered. He pushed deep again, shuddered and then brought his mouth to hers for a long slow kiss that tasted of contentment.

He laughed lightly, the sound not much more than a breath of air. "Not exactly what I had planned."

Jayne looped her arms around his neck. "What did you have planned?"

"Seduction, if you didn't toss me out on my ear before I had a chance. Something slow and irresistible."

"Well, you *were* irresistible," she said.

"And there's always later for slow."

"Mm-hmm."

Jayne held him, with her arms and her legs, amazed by the power of the way they'd come together, so quickly and completely. "I was afraid you wouldn't come back and I'd never get the chance to tell you—"

"Jayne," he said, a warning in his voice.

"—that I'm sorry," she finished. Had he been afraid she'd declare her love again? He'd certainly tried to silence her. Why was he so afraid? "I heard you talking to Marsh and I...for a little while I believed that you were—"

"It doesn't matter now," he interrupted.

"It does," Jayne whispered. "I didn't trust my heart. I didn't trust you. I'm so sorry."

He kissed her quickly. "It's okay, sugar."

"How can you say that?"

He pushed her nightgown higher, brushed his hand over her breasts, one and then the other. "Tonight we have better things to do than lie here and talk about everything we've done wrong. I want to get these clothes off. I want to make you scream again."

"Did I scream?"

"You did. For a second I thought maybe there was a snake in the bed."

"Very funny," she whispered. "But, Boone—" he silenced her with a kiss, and Jayne soon forgot all the confessions she'd been determined to make.

Boone reclined in the tub, eyes closed. A contented Jayne faced him, sitting between his spread legs and lazily washing him with a soapy washcloth. Warm water lapped around them both as she ran the washcloth up and down his thighs.

What was he going to do now? He couldn't follow Jayne around like a besotted puppy, and he could hardly ask her to come to Alabama with him. They still didn't have anything in common. Okay, they had one thing in common and it was pretty damn good, but sex alone did not a relationship make. It might be nice to try, though....

"Oh!" Jayne said, jumping slightly and splashing the water. "Corbin Marsh. Did you catch him? Was he shot? Is he in jail?"

Boone opened his eyes and pinned them on Jayne's beautiful face. "He got away."

Her eyes went wide. "He did?"

"Trap door in the closet that led to a tunnel. He was gone before we even knew it was there." His jaw clenched. "Marsh was Gurza."

The bewilderment on her face was genuine. Someone like Jayne would have a hard time understanding that level of deception. "How is that possible?"

Shock and Del were still astounded by this one, and it was going to make a great story, for the media and for those long nights when the guys were gathered around the bar. "According to Darryl, Marsh pulled Gurza out when he needed to scare someone. He had a black wig, brown contact lenses, some makeup and at least one set of clothes that might be considered common. He always set up meetings in dark places, where his face was never completely clear. Killed a guy once, slit his throat in front of a bunch of midlevel dealers just to make sure they stayed honest." He shook his head.

"How did Drew's mother meet him?"

Darryl had shared this, too, finally deciding to tell all and make whatever kind of deal he could. Shock had been very persuasive. "She showed up at a buy with a boyfriend, a dealer. Drew was in the back seat of this guy's car." Boone shook his head again, angry that anyone would involve a child in that world. "Marsh was apparently taken with Erin, and I think he was also appalled that the child was there. He took them home with him, leaving Darryl to finish up with the deal and dispose of Erin's boyfriend. Of course, it didn't take long for Erin to figure out that Gurza and Marsh were one and the same. That scared her. Marsh found out she was planning to run, so he shot her up with heroin and had Harvey dump her body in Flagstaff."

"A deal," Jayne whispered. "Does that mean Darryl will be getting out of jail soon?"

She'd always been afraid of Darryl. "Not for a very, very long time."

Jayne carefully crawled over his body, coming to rest her head on his wet chest. "Where is he now, do you think?" She shuddered.

"Far, far away," he said, hoping it was true. "Too many people in this part of the country know him. His face has been all over the news. He's running." Jayne sighed, and Boone rested his hand on her hair, flicking his fingers through the red-gold curls. "I never did thank you for saving my hide."

Jayne lifted her head. "Did I?"

"I didn't hear Harvey coming up with that gun."

Jayne licked her lips. "Well, if I did save your hide, it's only fair. You saved mine more than once." Her eyes, green with a touch of blue, sparkled. "You know, in some cultures, that would mean we...own each other. For the rest of our lives we are obligated to care for and watch over each other."

The rest of our lives. The concept scared him the way snakes scared Jayne. "Maybe we could start slow. How about just for tonight we care for and watch over, and we'll see how it goes."

Jayne smiled. "Deal." She pressed her mouth to his neck, flicked her tongue, moaned when he ran his hand down her wet back.

Boone got up, taking Jayne with him, and they both stepped out of the tub. They stood holding each other, the wet length of his body molded to hers. He was hard, ready again, but this time he was not going to give Jayne a quick, half-clothed tumble.

He grabbed a towel and began to dry her, gently, slowly, starting with her shapely back and working his way over her backside, down her thighs. He stopped only long enough to kiss her birthmark. She quivered in response.

That done, he turned her around and dried her front. Neck first, then shoulders, arms, hands. When they were dry, he lifted one arm and brushed his mouth over the sensitive skin at her inner elbow. Her breasts were next, and he was especially gentle here. He brushed the towel over her hard nipples, then followed with a lingering kiss to each one. Jayne closed her eyes, touched his hair and sighed. "Is this seduction?"

"Yes, ma'am," Boone said as he ran the towel from breasts to belly button.

"I like it," she whispered.

He dried Jayne's fine legs, starting with her ankles and working his way up to her thighs, gently urging her to part those thighs for him. He dropped the towel and pressed his mouth to her most intimate place, briefly, arousing her and then moving away. Going back to touch her again.

Jayne shuddered, took a deep breath and opened her eyes as Boone stood up. "My turn?"

She dried him much as he had her, her hands trembling, her fingers searching and her mouth stopping here and there to tease and arouse. She was tender and curious, and her smile...the sexy smile she gave him was enough to turn any man's insides to melted butter.

Hands so small and gentle had an unbelievably intoxicating effect on him. Just the sight of her pale fingers on his body was so arousing it made him want to take her here and now.

When he was dry, she knelt before him and took him in her mouth, touching and tasting with a sense of wonder at her newly discovered passion, a shyness mined with boldness that was absolutely intoxicating. She learned the size and shape of him with her hands and her mouth, and when she tilted her head back and looked up at him with hunger in her eyes, he growled, "Enough," and pulled her to her feet and then off them.

He carried her out of the bathroom, into the more gently lit bedroom of her suite. The sheets on the big bed were already twisted. The woman in his arms trembled with anticipation. And he wanted her in a way he had never wanted any other woman.

He laid Jayne on the bed and sat beside her, running

his hands over her thighs, leaning down to take a pebbled nipple deep into his mouth. Jayne closed her eyes and parted her thighs, wanting him as fiercely and completely as he wanted her.

Taking his hands and his mouth from Jayne was not what he had in mind, but he had to leave her long enough to fetch a condom from the back pocket of his jeans. He'd forgotten once; he couldn't let that happen again.

When he joined her in the bed, he hovered over her and kissed her deeply while he filled her, taking his time, relishing every second that passed, every heartbeat, every tremble. Every time he pushed in, she surged against him, her legs wrapped around his hips, her arms around his neck.

Time stopped, until there was nothing but these two bodies and the way they came together, joined and searching. They fit, physically and in another way he could not quite explain, in a way that would have scared him if he hadn't been so lost in sensation. If he hadn't been so enraptured by the heat and caress of her body.

He didn't want this night to end. Every time he sheathed himself inside this woman, she seemed to reach a new level of passion. This was pleasure, pure and simple, but it was more than that. It was an extraordinary moment in his ordinary life. One night so beautiful it made up for a thousand ugly nights that had come before.

Jayne whispered his name, rose into him and shattered beneath and around him. Her cry reached from down deep, captured him, and he came hard and fast.

Depleted, his body drifted down to cover hers, and he cradled her, protected her.

"I can't breathe," she whispered.

"Neither can I." Boone rested his forehead against hers.

"I'm going to die here," Jayne said softly, her hands stroking his hair. "Breathless and boneless and happy."

It hit Boone, in an unwelcome flash, that Jayne had been right. They did own each other, and it had nothing to do with him saving her life or her saving his. It just *was*, in a way that defied explanation, in a way that scared him so much he was tempted to get up, get dressed and leave without saying a word.

He wasn't usually such a coward.

After a short deep nap, Jayne awoke and found Boone lying beside her, wide awake and staring up at the ceiling. She rolled into him. "You should be sleeping."

"I know."

"What's wrong?" In her mind, nothing was wrong or ever would be again. This was right. She belonged with Boone and he with her, and that was all that mattered.

"I've just been…thinking."

She nestled her head against his chest. "Think tomorrow," she whispered. "Sleep tonight."

He rested his hand in her hair, possessive and loving. "I wish I could."

She held him, one bare body against another. "We'll talk it out, and then you can sleep."

"No…"

"It always helps to have someone to talk to when your mind is spinning this way and that." Her fingers carressed his back.

Boone sighed, but he didn't tense or move away.

"You asked me once why I specialize in looking for lost children."

Jayne wanted to prop herself up and see Boone's face, but she didn't. She simply burrowed her body more closely into his. "You didn't answer."

"I've never told anyone," he said softly. "Not my brothers, not my sister...no one."

She wanted him to tell her, to confide in her. To trust her. But she wasn't sure she deserved his trust, not yet. "You can tell me if you want."

For a few minutes he said nothing, and Jayne thought the conversation was over. She would not pressure him, nag or push him to share anything he wasn't ready to share. Maybe one day...

"I used to be a cop," he said. "Back in those days I was green, like every other rookie, and more ambitious than most. I had great plans. A stellar career, a detective, eventually homicide. I even had a regulation haircut, a patrol car and a uniform."

She could see him, Boone the policeman out to save the world.

"This one kid, a boy named Patrick, was constantly running away from home. I took the call from his folks several times. Other officers took other calls. The parents were always frantic, even though Patrick always came home when he thought they'd suffered enough." He shook his head. "The kid was a real pain in the ass," he added in a whisper.

"One day I got a call from that address. It had been a bad day, one of those days you think is never going to end. So I went in with an attitude. Hell, the boy was less than two months from his eighteenth birthday. Two months from being able to leave home legally."

Jayne kissed his chest gently, offering the only comfort she knew how to offer at the moment.

"His parents were frantic once again. Patrick hadn't come home. His mother was in tears, his father was wringing his hands, and I just snapped. I told them the boy would come home when he got hungry or bored or figured he'd made them suffer long enough. I told them he was a spoiled troublemaker and they should enjoy a few days of peace before the brat came home." Boone's breathing changed, became shallow. "I filed a report, but I didn't do anything. I didn't alert the other officers who were coming on shift to keep an eye out for the kid. I didn't drive around the neighborhood looking for him. I just…wrote him off."

She knew what was coming by the way Boone tensed beneath her.

"They found his body two days later. He'd been walking home from the store when he was hit by a car and thrown into an overgrown ditch. A soft drink was found close by, and he had a candy bar in his pocket. Candy! He was just a kid, and someone hit him and ran."

"You couldn't have known."

"They tell me he didn't die right away," Boone went on. "He lived in that ditch for hours, hurt and unable to move or make a sound. If I'd searched for him, if I'd done my job—"

"No." Jayne laid a hand on Boone's face and looked him in the eye. "What happened to that boy is not your fault."

"No," he whispered. "But if I'd searched for him, I might have found him and he might be alive today."

"Boone—"

"And what's even worse, while that kid was dying,

I stood there and told his parents that their only child was a pain in the ass and they were better off without him.''

"Honey—"

"And I have nightmares about Patrick, still. I will probably always have nightmares about him. I keep thinking that if I take enough kids home, if find decent homes for the ones who don't have a safe place to go back to, then maybe the nightmares will stop.'' He reached out and touched her face. "But I don't think they ever will. So it doesn't matter that I…like you more than I've ever liked any other woman. It doesn't matter that I want things I can't have. This is my life. This is all that matters to me.''

Jayne leaned over Boone and took his face in her hands. He loved her. Maybe he could only admit that he *liked* her, but he did love her. She kissed him tenderly. "Let me watch over you while you rest,'' she whispered. "I won't allow nightmares to invade your sleep. I'll watch and keep you safe, and when tomorrow morning comes—''

"Jayne—"

She wasn't going to allow him to silence her, not this time. "I will still love you.''

He gathered her against his chest, held her closely. Eventually he slept.

Chapter 18

The intrusive shrill ring of the phone woke her. Heavy curtains kept out the morning light, but the bedside clock told Jayne it was much later in the day than she normally slept.

"Boone?" The bed was empty. His clothes had been picked up off the floor. Even his jacket was gone. When she'd gone to sleep, it had been tossed across that empty chair by the window. The phone shrilled again and she reached out to snag it. "Hello?"

"Sweetheart, I'm in the lobby."

Jayne's heart sank as she glanced into the empty bathroom. Where was Boone? "Hi, Daddy."

"Did I wake you?" he asked, sounding surprised.

"Yes," she confessed, rolling from the bed. "Sorry. Yesterday was a really long day."

"I'll be up in two minutes."

"Wait!" Too late. Her father had disconnected and was on his way up.

Jayne grabbed her underwear and nightgown from the floor and put them in a dresser drawer with her other dirty clothes. Not having much time to dress before her father arrived, she chose a pale-green sundress that hung near the front of the closet. She had so much to say to her father, but at the moment only one thing was on her mind. Where was Boone? Surely he hadn't left. Surely last night meant more to him than goodbye.

As she stepped into her sandals, her father's familiar sharp knock sounded on the door. She ruffled her curls with her fingers as she went to let him in. There wasn't time for much else in the way of preparation. What was she going to say to him?

Hi, Daddy. Guess what? I met this man and you're going to love him as much as I do. No. Not good enough.

Daddy! Guess what happened to me! No. He might take that the wrong way.

Daddy, I'm in love. He loves me, I know he does, even though right now I have no idea where he is or if he's coming back...

Jayne opened the door. "Daddy..."

"Sweetheart." Gus Barrington swept into the room, gave Jayne a big hug and then set her away from him to look her up and down with the calculating eyes of a protective father. His number-one assistant, Chad, was one step behind him as usual. "You look wonderful, not a bit the worse for wear." His grin was stellar.

"Thanks."

Chad, who was thirty-five, thin and ambitious, and would never go far because he apparently could not smile at all, took over. "The press conference starts in twenty minutes."

"Press conference?" Jayne asked.

"The lobby is swarming with media, sweetheart," her father explained. "They have a hundred questions and I can't answer even one. It seemed best to just let Chad set something up and be done with it. I knew you wouldn't mind."

It was also free airtime, Jayne realized with a sigh.

Chad studied her. "The dress is lovely, Jayne, but a little casual for a press conference. Don't you have a suit handy? The muted red or the teal, I think."

Pamela always teased Jayne about traveling with so many clothes, but Jayne knew she had to be prepared for anything on the road. Even the unexpected press conference.

"Sure," she said, feeling more than a little disappointed. This wasn't exactly the warm reunion she had imagined.

Her father waved Chad off, and the assistant obediently stepped back. Unable to waste a single moment of his busy life, Chad opened his leather portfolio and began to leaf through the papers there. Surely something important needed to be done immediately.

Jayne stood very still while her father placed his hands on her shoulders and gazed down at her. "Are you really all right?" he asked. "You look fine, you really do, but from what little I've heard, I know you've been through a harrowing experience."

Jayne nodded. He had no idea. "Corbin Marsh was a drug dealer and a murderer. He planned to support you publicly and financially, and then…blackmail you into helping him." She shook her head. "If things had happened differently, if we hadn't found out who and what Marsh was, he could have dragged you into something very ugly."

She got a Gus Barrington grin for her concern.

"Don't worry about what might have happened. Truth be told, I would turn on a snake like that one in a heartbeat, even if it meant an end to my political career."

"I know that," she said softly. She occasionally got annoyed with the public aspect of her father's life, but he was a decent man who really did want to do good.

"Daddy, so much has happened. I don't know where to start." She shook her head softly. "And I don't know what to tell the press. In truth, I'd rather not talk to them at all. I will, if you need me there, but can we just tell them I'm fine and that we'll discuss what happened at a later date?"

She saw the concern in her father's eyes. "If that's what you want."

"Senator," Chad interjected, "the story will be cold in a few days, and this is such positive press…"

"If Jayne doesn't want to talk about what happened today, she doesn't have to." Her father smiled. "I'll tell them she's unhurt and safe and I'm taking her home. That will be good enough."

Jayne smiled. "Thank you," she said softly.

Another knock on the door. Boone! Oh, this was not the time to introduce the two most important men in her life.

"I ordered coffee," Chad said, heading for the door. "Wait…"

Her weak protest came too late. Chad opened the door, and the man who burst inside was not Boone and he was not delivering coffee. The intruder knocked Chad aside. Papers went flying, the leather portfolio fell to the floor and was kicked away by the man who stormed into the room, and Chad let out a weak squeal as he hit the floor.

Jayne didn't recognize him at first, this man with

black hair and swarthy skin. All she saw was the gun in his hand. When he looked directly at her, though, she knew. Apparently he'd left his brown contact lenses behind. The pale blue eyes looked eerie against the makeup-darkened skin.

"Marsh," she said.

"What a lovely picture the two of you make," he snarled. Marsh tried to slam the door behind him, but Chad's foot blocked it. A stunned Chad grunted as the door glanced off his ankle. Marsh seemed not to notice. "Father and child, reunited at last. How very moving." He glared at Jayne and cocked his head to one side. "Where is he?"

"I don't know what you're—"

Marsh raised the weapon and pointed it at her. "Sinclair, Becker, whatever you call him. *Where is he?*"

"Jayne?" Her father tried to place himself protectively in front of her. "Who is this man looking for?"

Marsh grinned and circled around, maintaining his distance and keeping the gun trained on her at all times. "Ah, he doesn't know yet, does he? The fireworks have not yet begun. I always thought it would be fun to watch the senator meet the lowlife his little girl has been screwing silly."

Gus Barrington tensed and took a step forward. "How dare you—"

"Daddy," Jayne said, stilling her father's progress with a steady hand. She gave Marsh her full attention. "I don't know where Boone is. He left."

Marsh/Gurza shook his head. "He was after the kid all along," he said. "I never saw it, not until it was too late. I cared about that child, you know. I truly did. His mother was a crackhead and a whore, but Drew was innocent. He was the only good thing in my life."

"How long would he have remained good?" Jayne snapped. "You would have poisoned him sooner or later. You would have turned him into another Darryl or another Harvey. He didn't have a chance at a decent life as long as he stayed with you."

Marsh shook the gun at her. "You helped him. You helped that no-good liar take Drew from me. You're going to pay for that." His hand steadied.

"If you fire that weapon, you'll never get out of this hotel alive," the senator said calmly.

Marsh swung his gaze to the senator. "My life is over. My home, Drew, my career—careers, I should say—my fortune…all gone. But I'm not going alone." He took aim at Jayne.

The door burst open. A blur of leather and denim, Boone jumped over Chad and threw himself in front of Jayne and her father as the gun went off. A surprised Marsh twitched at the last minute, and his aim was bad. The window behind Jayne and her father shattered.

Marsh didn't get off another shot before Boone knocked the gun aside, delivering an uppercut that spun Marsh around. The gun went flying, then skittered across the floor. Both men were now unarmed, and any sane person would know that Boone had the advantage, fighting hand to hand. He was younger and bigger. Still, an enraged Marsh rushed at Boone.

Boone spun once and kicked out, his booted foot catching Marsh in the chest and sending him reeling backward to fall on Chad. The senator's aide let out a breathy squeal before he came to his senses and gave the stunned Marsh a shove that sent him rolling back into the room.

Once more Marsh tried to stand, but he didn't have anything left. Boone wrestled the desperate man down, face pressed into the carpet. When he had Marsh pinned to the floor, Boone looked up at Jayne. He took a long deep breath.

"Call room 819, sugar, and tell Shock if he hurries, I'll let him put handcuffs on the bogeyman."

All he really wanted was to touch Jayne and make sure she was okay. She looked fine, if a little pale, but he wanted to hold her close and judge for himself.

That wasn't going to happen anytime soon. She'd been hustled off by her father to prepare for the press conference that had been unavoidably delayed. The gunshot had brought everyone running. There was no canceling the press conference now, according to Jayne's father.

Once Boone had handed Corbin Marsh over to Del and Shock, he'd been left momentarily alone with the senator and the pipsqueak he'd had to leap over to get into Jayne's room. You could cut the tension in the air with a knife, and if he could've run without looking like a complete coward, he most definitely would have.

He'd returned to Jayne's room to say goodbye, never expecting that he'd hear Marsh's angry voice drifting through the partially open door. He didn't want to think about what might have happened if he hadn't come back to say goodbye.

The pipsqueak kept insisting that they include Boone in the press conference. Some nonsense about the common man risking his life, blah, blah, blah. The senator, on the other hand, stared at Boone as if he wanted to take him apart, one piece at a time. What had Jayne told him?

What difference did it make? Even a little bit of the truth would cause the senator to look at him this way.

Jayne emerged from the bedroom looking beautiful as always, if a little formal in her pearls and pale-blue-green suit. He tried to talk to her, but the pipsqueak hurried her along and out of Boone's reach. He followed, not because he had anything to say to the damned press, but because he still hadn't spoken with Jayne.

And like it or not, he did have to tell her goodbye. After he'd dropped the Pattersons and Lacey off at the airport, he'd considered just heading home, too. Back to Alabama. On to the next case. But Jayne wasn't a woman you walked away from without a word.

A part of him wanted to keep her a while longer. Another part knew this would never last.

In the elevator she scooted close to him. "Where were you?" she whispered.

He leaned down slightly. "I took Drew and his grandparents to the airport." Since her father was present, he didn't tell her that he hadn't wanted to wake her, she'd looked so peaceful.

"The Pattersons seem very nice." She reached out and laid her hand on his arm, a move the senator followed with great interest. "Drew will be happy there."

He couldn't believe he had told Jayne about Patrick and the nightmares. She must think him such a fool, to feel guilty even now, to be too stubborn to let an old mistake go. He had never told anyone before, had never even been tempted. Patrick was his dark secret to keep, his nightmare to bear. You didn't share your nightmares with just anyone. You didn't tell all just because for a little while, having someone to share your burden with made it lighter.

Jayne didn't need his burdens. No one did.

The lobby came too soon, and they were rushed

through a small crowd to a meeting room where cameras, reporters and microphones awaited the senator's arrival.

Boone stopped by the door. The senator took Jayne's arm and they moved up the aisle, smiling. Very much in control. Jayne looked back once and urged Boone forward with a nod of her head. He shook his head and stayed put.

The pipsqueak informed the reporters about Marsh's assassination attempt, and how a man—he indicated Boone with a wave of his hand—had bravely thrown himself between the senator and a bullet.

Heads turned. Lights hit Boone in the face. Curious eyes turned to him for answers. Hell, he didn't belong here. What was he thinking? Goodbyes were for sweethearts. He and Jayne had never been anything but lovers. Lovers could walk away.

The reporters bombarded him with questions he ignored. They held out microphones and aimed cameras in his direction. Jayne watched from the small raised dais at the far front of the room, where she stood beside her father. If ever he needed a reminder that they came from different worlds...

Finally one voice rose above the rest. "What compelled you to throw yourself in front of the senator?"

Boone shook his head. "I didn't throw myself in front of the senator." With that he turned around and pushed his way through the door.

Jayne's heart stopped as the doors closed behind Boone and the cameras and reporters turned this way once again. No, he hadn't thrown himself in front of the senator. He had thrown himself in front of *her*. And now he was walking away. She'd seen his face before he'd turned around. It wasn't the face of a man who'd be waiting in the lobby when the press conference was done.

Jayne edged toward the stairs as her father stood tall at the podium. "I'll be happy to answer any questions," he began.

Chad made a hissing sound and tried to wave Jayne back to her post behind her father, and the senator glanced her way as she stepped down the stairs.

"Sorry, Daddy," she whispered. "I have to go."

She didn't wait for a response, but hurried down the stairs and headed for the door. Halfway down the aisle, she began to run. Eyes and cameras followed, but she didn't pay them any mind.

She burst through the doors into the lobby and immediately saw Clint and Dean standing just a few feet away, their luggage at their feet as if they were waiting for a ride to the airport.

"Where is he?" she asked breathlessly.

"Miss Barrington," Dean began almost solemnly. "This really isn't a good—"

"Not now, big brother." Wearing a wide grin, Clint pointed to the revolving door. "He went thataway."

Jayne took a step and then heard the door behind her open. She spun on Boone's brothers. "A reporter or two might try to follow me," she said as she backed toward the revolving door. "Do me a favor and don't let them."

"We can't waylay reporters in the lobby," Dean protested.

"Why not?" Clint asked, cracking his knuckles and then giving his neck a twist that made something there crack, as well.

Jayne didn't wait to see what would happen. She

turned away and ran for the revolving glass door, her eyes already searching the front drive and the parking lot beyond. She looked for a leather jacket and a head of long brown hair, but she saw nothing. What if she was too late?

She ran into the parking lot, stopping once to spin around. It was such a beautiful day. The sky was impossibly blue, the air touched with spring. How could such a terrible thing happen on such a beautiful day? It wasn't right.

Boone was nowhere to be seen. Well, she could find her way to Birmingham if she had to, and she imagined that since Boone had a business there, she'd be able to find him. But she didn't want to wait. She didn't want to spend hours on a plane wondering if he would be there, if he would be glad to see her. She wanted to see him now!

Jayne spun one more time and he was there, stalking toward her from the three-story garage situated at the far end of the parking lot. When her eyes lit on him, she stood still and waited a moment, then ran to meet him.

"What are you doing?" Boone asked when they both came to a stop, three feet apart.

"Chasing you," Jayne said. "My grandmother would be horrified." She explained, "Nice girls don't chase men in the parking lot or anywhere else."

"Then maybe you'd better get back inside and finish your press conference." For some reason those words made his jaw clench.

"Daddy will be fine on his own. This is more important." She glanced back at the hotel. So far not a single reporter had followed her through that door. Getting past Clint and Dean would be difficult, but still, if the reporters were determined to follow, she didn't exactly have all the time in the world.

She returned her gaze to Boone, shading her eyes with one hand so she could see his face clearly. "Do you love me?"

"I'm pretty sure Granny wouldn't like that, either," Boone said, his jaw relaxing a little. "Surely nice girls don't go around—"

"Dammit, Boone!"

His eyebrows lifted slightly. "Jayne Barrington, did you just say dammit?"

Jayne felt the warm blush in her face, but she didn't back down. She knew what Boone was doing. He was trying to make light of what had happened. He was trying to laugh off this moment so he could walk away with a clear conscience.

"Fine," she said softly. "You think I should go back inside? All you have to do is tell me you don't love me."

Again his face and his eyes went hard.

"Should be easy enough for you," she said. "It's what you do best. You lie. Lie now and tell me you don't love me, and I'll walk away, and when the reporters ask me who you are, I'll tell them you're just some nice man who saved my life a couple of times." She took a step forward. "Or tell the truth for once. Tell me you love me, and we'll walk out of here together right now. I'll work with you, if that's what you want. I'll help you find lost children and chase away nightmares. Or I'll wait for you while you do what you have to, if you need to do it alone, and then I'll be there for you when you come home."

"Jayne, this is—"

"No. No more arguments, no more jokes. The lie or the truth. Your choice."

Boone took a deep breath. "I don't..." The rest of the sentence stuck in his throat.

Jayne didn't say a word; she simply looked at him and waited.

"I can't..."

He couldn't lie to her, she knew it.

Boone grabbed her wrist and pulled her to him. She raised her arms to encircle his neck while he lifted her off her feet and hugged her tightly. "Of course I love you, dammit," he growled. "But that doesn't mean it's going to work. You should be with someone who... who...someone like that pipsqueak in there. The little guy with the clipboard and the pocket protector."

"Chad?" she asked, horrified.

"Whatever," he grumbled.

Jayne kissed Boone's neck and threaded her fingers through his hair. "But I love you. And we need each other. We own each other, deep inside where no one else will ever see."

"I know." He sighed, his entire body relaxed.

"I love *you*."

Boone held her close. "I don't ever want to let you go," he whispered. "I don't want you out of my sight for five minutes."

"Afraid I'll get in trouble again?" she teased.

He had looked at her this way before, eyes dark and hooded, lips tempting and slightly parted, neck corded with tension. "No. The truth is, I don't have anything real and good without you. That's scary for a guy who never needed anything before."

"You need me."

"Darn straight I do."

"I need you, too," she confessed. "Like I need air and water and sleep."

"Then I guess you'll have to marry me," he said gruffly.

"I guess I will."

Boone smiled. He kissed her deep and long. And when he took his mouth from hers, he whispered, "Yee-haw."

Epilogue

Summer in Mississippi. Sunday dinner. A father-in-law who didn't like him much, a mother-in-law who was still pouting because there hadn't been a big wedding, and a grandmother-in-law who was determined to feed him until he literally burst. To Boone's way of thinking, chasing bad guys was much easier.

Jayne rolled into him and woke up slowly, and with a smile. They'd spent the night here in Hooker Bend, Mississippi, sleeping in the bed where Jayne had grown up. It was a double bed, not a king like they had at home, and the old thing was noisy as hell. Everyone in the house surely knew when he so much as turned over in the night. He hated antiques, and this house was filled with them.

"Good morning," she whispered.

Boone kissed his wife. "Good morning."

Her mother had not been happy that they'd flown to Vegas and been married by an Elvis impersonator, but when they'd started talking weddings and Jayne's mother had mentioned a year of planning, it had seemed like a good idea.

No way had he been willing to wait a year to make Jayne his wife.

Her smile was warm. "I dreamed about babies," she said, sighing. "Your nephew was so cute."

"*Our* nephew." Their two-day visit to Atlanta had been quick. Shea and Jayne had hit it off, as he'd known they would. Everyone loved Jayne. What was not to love? Boone was so content these days he hadn't even wanted to slug Clint when his little brother lifted the new baby and introduced him to Uncle BooBoo.

Boone had been surprised by the intensity of the emotions seeing that baby had triggered. Justin Taggert, now three days old, was a part of the family now. Someone else to watch over and protect, another person to draw into the close circle. How could you fall in love with a tiny wiggling thing that couldn't speak, smile or fend for itself in even the smallest way?

"How many do you want?" he asked. A short time ago the idea of being a father had terrified him. Now…it seemed right.

"Babies?"

"What else?"

Jayne snuggled close and murmured. "I haven't decided. More than one, for sure. I always hated being an only child. Maybe we should have three or four." She smiled. "Three boys and a girl."

"Three girls and a boy," he countered. He rolled on top of Jayne. The bed creaked like it was about to fall apart.

Jayne laughed softly and raked her fingers through his hair.

Her father the senator, who insisted that Boone call him Gus, had invited Boone into his office last night after dinner and offered him twenty thousand dollars to cut his hair. After an appropriately vulgar response, Boone had told the senator that if Jayne ever asked him to cut his hair, he'd do it, and it wouldn't cost anyone a dime.

He didn't think Gus was going to love having a Sinclair as a son-in-law. After all, Boone's family included a rodeo clown, a reporter who liked to stir up trouble and her once-convicted-of-murder husband. And him. He was used to being a black sheep and didn't mind carrying on the tradition to a new family. Besides, there was always Dean to smooth things over.

Things had not gotten off to a great start. A wily photographer, who had slipped past Clint while he was hog-tying a reporter, had taken a picture of Jayne and Boone in the Flagstaff hotel parking lot a little more than a month ago. The photograph had made quite a few papers. They'd been kissing. He had been holding Jayne off her feet at the time, and her skirt had ridden up a little. It wasn't scandalous by any means, but Jayne had shown a lot more thigh than usual. The senator had hated the picture, according to Jayne.

Boone had framed one and hung it on his office wall.

"Are you ready for this?" Jayne whispered.

Boone rocked his body against hers. The bed squeaked. At this rate they were going to end up on the floor. Which also squeaked, but not as much.

His wife smiled. He loved her smile. "Not that," she whispered. "Babies. In-laws. Sunday dinner. Forever."

"Yes."

"No doubts?"

"I took an oath before Elvis," he reminded her. "For better or for worse."

"So far it's all been better." She hooked one leg around his.

"I love you," he said. "When the worse comes, we'll be ready."

She didn't argue with him and try to tell him their days would all be sunshine and roses. Occasionally there would be sunburn and thorns. There would be nightmares and failures, along with the joys and successes. That was life. It was real. *This* was real.

Jayne was more than his lover, more than his wife. She was his partner in every way.

And she owned him from the heart out.

Yee-haw.

* * * * *

Later on this year Del gets a blast from the past. Stay tuned for Linda Winstead Jones's next Intimate Moments!

INTIMATE MOMENTS™

presents:

Romancing the Crown

With the help of their powerful allies, the royal family of Montebello is determined to find their missing heir. But the search for the beloved prince is not without danger—or passion!

Available in July 2002:
HER LORD PROTECTOR
by Eileen Wilks (IM #1160)

When Rosie Giaberti has a psychic vision about the missing prince of Montebello, she finds herself under the protection of dashing Lord Drew Harrington. But will the handsome royal keep her secrets—and her heart—safe?

This exciting series continues throughout the year with these fabulous titles:

Available only from Silhouette Intimate Moments
at your favorite retail outlet.

Where love comes alive™

Visit Silhouette at www.eHarlequin.com

SIMRC7

Discover the secrets of
CODE NAME: DANGER

in

MERLINE LOVELACE'S

thrilling duo

DANGEROUS TO KNOW

When tricky situations need a cool head, quick wits and a touch of ruthlessness, Adam Ridgeway, director of the top secret OMEGA agency, sends in his team. Lately, though, his agents have had romantic troubles of their own....

UNDERCOVER MAN & PERFECT DOUBLE

And don't miss
TEXAS HERO
(IM #1165, 8/02)
which features the newest OMEGA adventure!

If you liked this set of stories, be sure to find
DANGEROUS TO HOLD.
*Available from your local retailer
or at our online bookstore.*

Silhouette®

Where love comes alive™

Visit Silhouette at www.eHarlequin.com

PSDTK

CROWN AND GLORY

**Where royalty and romance
go hand in hand...**

The series continues in Silhouette Romance
with these unforgettable novels:

HER ROYAL HUSBAND
by Cara Colter
on sale July 2002 (SR #1600)

THE PRINCESS HAS AMNESIA!
by Patricia Thayer
on sale August 2002 (SR #1606)

SEARCHING FOR HER PRINCE
by Karen Rose Smith
on sale September 2002 (SR #1612)

And look for more Crown and Glory stories in
SILHOUETTE DESIRE starting in October 2002!

Available at your favorite retail outlet.

Silhouette®
Where love comes alive™

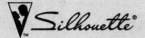

COMING NEXT MONTH

#1159 LAWMAN'S REDEMPTION—Marilyn Pappano
Heartbreak Canyon
Canyon County Undersheriff Brady Marshall hadn't planned on fatherhood, but when fourteen-year-old Les came to town claiming to be his daughter, his plans changed. Alone and in danger, Les needed help and—more important—a family. And Brady needed his old flame Hallie Madison to make that happen....

#1160 HER LORD PROTECTOR—Eileen Wilks
Romancing the Crown
Visions of a troubled woman had haunted psychic Rosalinda Giaberti's mind ever since the moment she first saw the prince of Montebello. Rosie wanted to warn him, but there were those who would stop at nothing to keep her from him. It was up to Lord Drew Harrington to protect Rosie, but could he do that without risking his own heart?

#1161 THE BLACK SHEEP'S BABY—Kathleen Creighton
Into the Heartland
When Eric Lanagan came home for Christmas with an infant daughter, his family was shocked! They didn't know about the baby's true parents or her tragic past—a past shared by her aunt, Devon O'Rourke. Eric was falling in love with Devon, and he knew that the only way to keep his daughter was to make Devon remember the childhood she'd worked so hard to forget....

#1162 COWBOY UNDER COVER—Marilyn Tracy
Who was terrorizing the New Mexico ranch that city slicker Jeannie Wasserman had bought as a home for orphans? Undercover federal marshal Chance Salazar was sure it was the elusive *El Patrón*. Determined to catch his criminal, Chance got hired on as a cowboy and was prepared for anything—except his growing desire for Jeannie.

#1163 SWEET REVENGE—Nina Bruhns
Muse Summerfield was the hottest thing in New Orleans—until she disappeared. That was when her twin sister, Grace, and police detective Auri "Creole" Levalois began burning up Bourbon Street in an effort to find her. Creole believed that Muse held the key to his foster brother's murder, but would he and Grace survive their search?

#1164 BACHELOR IN BLUE JEANS—Lauren Nichols
High school sweethearts Kristin Chase and Zach Davis once had big dreams for their future, dreams that never came to pass. Years later, a suspicious death in their hometown brought Zach and Kristin back together. Surrounded by mystery and danger, they realized that they needed each other now more than ever.

SIMCNM0602